THREE-POINT PLAY

BOOK 6

Other Books in the
Spirit of the Game Series

THREE-POINT PLAY

BOOK 6

BY TODD HAFER

zonderkidz

The children's group of Zondervan

www.zonderkidz.com

Three-Point Play
Copyright ® 2005 by Todd Hafer

Requests for information should be addressed to
Zonderkidz, Grand Rapids, Michigan 49530

Library of Congress Cataloging-in-Publication Data

Hafer, Todd.
  Three-point play / Todd Hafer. – 1st ed.
    p. cm. – (Spirit of the game series ; bk. 6)
    Summary: During his freshman year of high school, Cody learns
lessons about leadership and teamwork while playing football and
basketball and while coping with his widower father's remarriage.
    ISBN-10: 0-310-70795-1 (softcover)
    ISBN-13: 978-0-310-70795-0
  [1. Christian life—Fiction. 2. Football—Fiction. 3. Basketball—
Fiction. 4. Leadership—Fiction. 5. Remarriage—Fiction.
6. Conduct of life—Fiction. 7. High schools—Fiction 8. Schools—
Fiction.]   I. Title. II. Series: Hafer, Todd. Spirit of the game series ;
bk. 6
  PZ7.H11975Thr 2005
  [Fic]–dc22
                                                    2005006501

Cover design by Alan Close
Interior design: Susan Ambs
Art direction: Laura Maitner–Mason
Photos by Synergy Photographic

Printed in the United States of America

05 06 07 08 09/DCI/5 4 3 2 1

Contents

To the life and memory of Tim Hanson,
a true athlete, a true friend.

Foreword

I love sports. I have always loved sports. I have competed in various sports at various levels, right through college. And today, even though my official competitive days are behind me, you can still find me on the golf course working on my game, or on a basketball court playing a game of pick-up.

Sports have also helped me learn some of life's important lessons—lessons about humility, risk, dedication, teamwork, and friendship. Cody Martin, the central character in the Spirit of the Game series, learns these lessons too. Some of them the hard way. I think you'll enjoy following Cody in his athletic endeavors.

Like most of us, he doesn't win every game or every race. He's not the best athlete in his school, not by a long shot. But he does taste victory because, as you'll see, he comes to understand that life's greatest victories aren't reflected on a scoreboard. They are the times when you rely on a strength beyond your own—a spiritual strength—to carry you through. They are the times when you put the needs of someone else before your own. They are the times when sports becomes a way to celebrate the life God has given you.

So read on, and may you always possess the true Spirit of the Game.

                           Toby McKeehan

Chapter 1

Unfinished Business

Cody Martin smiled as he walked past the Grant High School gym. *Ah, the sights and sounds of basketball practice,* he thought. *You gotta love 'em.*

He stopped momentarily at the south gym doorway and surveyed the flurry of activity: the rat-a-tat slapping of leather on hardwood as Terry Alston showed off his dribbling skills near the south baseline. The clang of Greg "the Cannon" Gannon's high-arcing jump shots as he tried to find his range from twenty feet. The squeaking of Terrance Dylan's shoes as he ran agility drills along the east sideline. Taking stock of it all was Coach Clayton, who had moved up from his Grant

Middle School position to lead the Eagle freshmen. The loose-limbed coach prowled the near sideline sporting a brand-new blue and silver warm-up suit, offering such helpful pointers as, "For the love of Rick Barry, will you puh-leeze concentrate when you shoot free throws, Mr. Matt Slaven?"

It was 6:25 in the morning on the second Monday of November, five minutes before the first frosh basketball practice. Gannon launched an air ball and almost ran into Cody as he scrambled to retrieve it.

"Hey, Martin," he panted. "You gonna join us this morning?"

Cody wagged his head. "Uh, Gannon, it's still football season for me. Second round of the play-offs are this Friday, in case you haven't heard."

Gannon shrugged. "I know. I just thought you might put in double duty. You know, run with us in the mornings, do football in the afternoons."

"Did a basketball hit you in the head, dude?" Cody asked with a chuckle. "I'm so sore I'm walking like Frankenstein. That's why I'm here so early. Gonna take a whirlpool, gonna have Dutch help me with some stretching."

"Well, I wish you guys well," Gannon said. "But we're gonna miss you. And Pork Chop, too. It rocks that you're both playing varsity football as freshmen. But we're thin without you. Especially on defense. We need some stoppers like you and the big fella. What's Porter weighing now, anyway? About 225? We could use that beef under the boards."

Cody turned to the locker room. "Hey, I hope we're out here with you soon," he said. "But not *too* soon."

With an involuntary groan, Cody slowly lowered himself into the bubbling water of the stainless steel whirlpool tub in the training room. *I wonder if there's any part of me that* doesn't *hurt.* He considered the question for a moment. *Maybe my hair. And I think my ears are okay.*

As he felt his aching muscles begin to relax, he leaned his head back and replayed the highlights of the Grant Eagles' win in the opening round of the Colorado high school football play-offs, just two days before.

Bishop Moreland was a Catholic school in the southern part of the state. Cody and his teammates had watched a video tape on them during their lunch hours leading up to the game. The Bulldogs were huge, but they looked a bit slow. Their offensive line didn't explode off the snap the way Pork Chop and his O-line teammates did.

On the other hand, Moreland had a 230-pound fullback named Michaels who played like a human battering ram. *If that guy breaks through the line and into the secondary,* Cody thought with a shudder the first time he saw Michaels on tape, *I don't know how I'm supposed to bring him down. He weighs twice as much as I do!*

Fortunately for Cody, when game day arrived the Eagles stacked their defense against the run, putting five players on the line with three linebackers playing tight behind them. That meant only three defensive backs, making Cody the odd DB out. He entered the game on likely passing downs, but even in these situations, the Bulldogs favored sending Michaels into the teeth of the Grant defense.

Watching most of the first half from the sidelines, Cody couldn't understand the strategy. The middle of the Grant line was occupied by Gordon "ATV" Daniels, a 210-pound tank who bench-pressed 340 pounds and owned legs like tree trunks.

Playing right behind ATV was Brendan Clark, among the state's best middle linebackers. He was a fierce hitter, and Cody felt himself cringing every time Clark collided with Michaels. The big fullback had more than thirty pounds on Clark, but more often than not, the latter stopped him cold.

The first half ended with the Eagles up 7–0. ATV, who was an even better fullback than a D-lineman, rumbled up the middle for a thirty-eight-yard touchdown run late in the second quarter to give the home team the edge.

After cups of Gatorade had been guzzled and a few ankles re-taped, Coach Martin Morgan gathered the team around him in the locker room. "You've seen the tapes," he said evenly. "You know what they're gonna do—keep blasting Michaels up the middle, hoping to wear us down physically and mentally. Most teams can't stop that big bruiser for a whole game. But you're not most teams. You keep plugging up the middle, and they're gonna get desperate. And that's when we slam the door on 'em."

ATV stood and began slamming the door of a locker behind him. Such was his power that Cody feared the door would fly off its hinges.

"Slam the door!" ATV bellowed after each effort. "Slam! Slam! Slam! Game over!"

Cody saw Coach Morgan catch the eye of Coach Curtis, one of his assistants. The latter flashed a quick smile and wagged his head admiringly. Since joining the varsity earlier in the season, Cody had found himself understanding football better and better each week. He had come to appreciate that motivating players was a huge part of a coach's job. *That must be why the coaches love a guy like ATV*, he thought. *I'm pretty sure he was* born *motivated!*

Neither team was able to generate much offense in the third quarter. Bryce Phillips, the Eagles' best wideout, picked up fifteen yards on an end-around, but as he struggled to churn out a few extra yards, he fumbled near midfield, halting Grant's only promising drive of the quarter.

The Bulldogs took over and, for the first time in the game, sent in two wideouts. "Okay," Coach Curtis barked. "Standard defense in—now! Two safeties, two corners!"

Cody swallowed hard as he buckled his chin strap and slid in his teeth guard.

He lined up at cornerback against number 84, a lanky wide receiver on the weak side (opposite the tight end) of the Bulldog line. As the center hiked the ball, the receiver charged at Cody, growling and snarling like an angry beast.

Cody held his ground, sending 84 a telepathic message: *All that noise might have worked against me early in the season, dude. But since then I've been growled at, screamed at, cussed at, and threatened by all kinds of guys bigger than me. So you're gonna have to bring something more than noise.*

Cody raised his arms and chucked 84 hard across the shoulder pads, then stepped inside him as he saw Michaels slide off-tackle and rumble upfield. Clark leaped on Michaels' back, swiping at the football, which the Bulldog runner held tucked in his right arm.

Oh, boy, Cody thought, as he saw the play develop, *here goes. This is gonna be like throwing myself under a truck or something.*

He angled in on Michaels, who was moving pretty well for a guy toting a fierce middle linebacker on his back. Cody dipped his left shoulder, getting as low as he could.

He held his breath as he sensed that the thrashing bulk of humanity was about to stumble over the top of him. *Please don't let Michaels step on me*, he prayed fervently, eyes closed tight.

Less than a second later, the impact came. He felt a sharp *thwack* as his left shoulder pad drove into something. *Either a fence post or Michaels' shinbone*, Cody reasoned. The force of the blow threatened to drive his shoulder blade down into his rib cage, but then the pressure and pain disappeared as quickly as they had come. There was the sound of a mini buffalo stampede rumbling over him, then a desperate groan erupting deep from within the chest of either Michaels or Clark.

Lying flat on his stomach, Cody turned to see Michaels falling, Clark still on his back and still chopping desperately at the ball. The duo hit the turf with a thud.

Clark quickly scrambled to his feet and head-butted Cody so hard that he thought his helmet might fly from his head. "That's the way to get low, Martin!" the linebacker roared. "That's the way to have my back!"

Cody tried to reign in his smile for a moment, then gave up. "That was cool—an assist on the tackle," he whispered to himself. "And I'm still alive! I can't believe it!"

Bishop Moreland picked up twelve yards on the play, so Cody wasn't surprised when they ran it once more. This time, 84, growling and snarling again, tried to block him high across the shoulder pads. Cody ducked under the block. ATV had snagged Michaels by an ankle, but the fullback, with a Neanderthal grunt, pulled free. Still, he was slowed enough for Clark to get to him, grabbing him around the waist this time.

Michaels charged forward, trying to fling Clark off of him. As Cody closed in, it looked like the fullback might be successful. Clark seemed to be losing his grip.

In desperation, Clark clawed at the ball as he began to slide off of Michaels. Cody saw Michaels counter the effort, switching the ball from his right arm to his left.

Cody reacted instinctively. He knew it was instinct, because logic would have told him to run to the sidelines right away to avoid being trampled again. (Then turn in his football uniform, grab a clarinet, and join the marching band.) He saw the ball, moving in what seemed like slow motion. He swiped at it with both hands, bringing his arms down with all the force he could summon.

Just before Michaels hit him flush in the chest, Cody saw the ball tumble to the ground.

Cody lay stunned, staring up at a near-cloudless sky. *Okay*, he thought, *my breathing can resume any day now—*

This was football's scariest moment. On your back, afraid to move. Afraid of lifting an arm or leg and feeling that sharp dagger of pain that meant a serious injury. Or struggling to stand, putting weight on one leg, then feeling an ankle or knee crumple like it was made of foam rubber.

Cody blinked as he saw someone standing over him. For a second, he thought it might be an angel, but then he realized that angels didn't wear eye-black—and, most likely, didn't sport two days' worth of razor stubble. Clark extended an arm. "You okay, Code?"

"That's a good question," Cody gasped. "Hey, how's Michaels? I didn't hurt him, did I?"

"Ha!" bellowed ATV, who had joined Clark. "You're something else, little man." He extended an arm too.

Tentatively, Cody lifted an arm toward each teammate. He marveled at the ease with which they pulled him to his feet.

"Everything intact, dude?" ATV asked.

Cody shifted his weight to his left foot, then his right. Then he rotated his head in a slow, clockwise circle. "Yeah," he said, noting the genuine surprise in his voice. "I think I'm okay."

He saw Dutch and Coach Curtis jogging toward him. He waved the trainer and coach off, then gave a double thumbs-up.

He turned to Clark. "You think they'll run off-tackle this next play?" he asked sarcastically.

Clark smiled cryptically. "Not this next play, that's for sure."

Cody cocked his head. "What makes you so certain?"

Clark gestured to the scoreboard, which now read Grant—13, Visitor—0. "Berringer was all over the fumble you forced, my man. He was in the end zone before any of the Moreland guys figured out what happened. You mighta just made the play of the game! Now, get off the field so we can boot the extra point."

As the game clock ticked down to 3:58, the Bulldogs' sense of desperation grew. They couldn't afford to send Michaels up the middle any more, as it would burn too much time off the clock, so they tried to scoot him around the ends so that he could run out of bounds and stop the clock. But Grant's pursuit was too good. And Michaels was strictly a north-and-south runner. He couldn't build up that frightening momentum while running laterally, and Clark bulldozed him on play after play.

On the Bulldogs' second-to-last possession of the game, number 84 (whom Cody had nicknamed Wolfman) beat him on a slant pattern. But Berringer, who was playing deep safety twenty yards from the line of scrimmage, came up to knock Wolfman's stilt-like legs out from under him.

The Bishop Moreland drive stalled at midfield with less than two minutes left in the game. Rather than go for a desperation fourth-down toss into the end zone, the Bulldogs punted, pinning the Eagles deep in their own territory, at the twelve.

Three straight running plays netted only eight yards for Grant—but forced the Bulldogs to relinquish all their time-outs.

A booming punt from ATV sailed over the head of the Bulldog return man and bounced and rolled all the way to the Bishop Moreland thirty. By the time the returner tracked down the ball, the Eagle pursuit was on him. Led by Clark, they held a team meeting on his body.

Wolfman beat Cody on a fade route on first down, moving his team to midfield. On second down, Moreland set Wolfman over the middle. Cody felt panic splash over him as he squared himself to put a hit on his much larger opponent. *Great,* he thought, *they're picking on me. That's great—go after the littlest guy on the field, why don't you!*

Cody was giving Wolfman plenty of cushion. He saw the ball streaking toward the receiver. He hoped he could time his hit so that he wouldn't be whistled for pass interference.

He needn't have worried. Clark had dropped back into coverage. He timed his leap perfectly and intercepted the pass at the Eagle thirty-five. He mashed the ball into the turf. "Game over," he said emphatically.

Cody joined Clark as they trotted off the field, smiling as he saw the Grant fans on their feet, screaming and clapping. "Thanks, Clark," he said. "Guess those guys decided their best chance for a comeback was to pick on the 140-pound freshman."

Clark shook his head. "You saved my bacon a while ago. I was just returning the favor. Besides, you had the coverage. You woulda dropped him if I hadn't gotten the pick."

Cody pondered the statement. *I'd like to* think *I would have,* he confessed to himself. *But that was one big Wolfman!*

Chapter 2

Haunted ...

Here's to you, my little brutha," Pork Chop said, raising his large chocolate milk shake in a toast. "To a skinny frosh who's bad enough to play varsity football. Varsity *play-off* football. And forcing a fumble from that brute Michaels? That was fierce, dawg. That brother's a load!"

Cody lifted his medium strawberry shake and nudged his cup against his friend's. It was Tuesday evening, time for the traditional Cody Martin/Pork Chop Porter football summit at the Dairy Delight.

"Thanks for the props, Chop," Cody said. "Sometimes I still can't believe this is real. I didn't even think I'd make the JV team this year. But varsity? It's like a dream. But a good dream, which is a nice change from all the bad ones I still have."

Chop took a long pull from the two straws he had plunged into his shake only moments ago. "Bad dreams, huh? Like what?"

Cody sighed. "Well, some of them are bad dreams, others are more like—sad dreams, I guess. Like, I can't help thinking how proud Mom would be if she were still alive, sitting in the stands and watching. I mean, it's the second round of the play-offs this weekend. I'd give anything for her to be able to see that."

"She can see you, dawg. I just know she can." Pork Chop's voice was uncharacteristically soft.

Cody tilted his head toward the ceiling. "I hope so," he whispered.

Chop plucked a french fry from the platter that sat between them. "So, dawg," he began, "that explains the sad dreams. What about the bad dreams?"

Cody whistled through his teeth. "I'm not even sure where to start on that subject. I mean, do you realize that it's less than a month before my dad and Beth get married? It didn't seem quite real when they first told me. But now that they've set a date, December second, I realize it's actually going to happen. It's just too weird: Beth is going to be living in *my* house. Cooking with my mom's pots and pans and stuff. Sleeping in my mom's bed. She wants to be a parent to me. I don't know how I'm gonna handle that. I don't even know what I'm supposed to call her. Dad wants me to call her Mom already. He gets mad when I call her Beth. Or just plain old You.

"Why don't you take my suggestion? Call her Backup Mama?"

Cody laughed sadly. "Yeah, right." He sat back in his side of the booth and let himself slouch. His mom, Linda Martin—his real mom—would have corrected him immediately for that. "You have a nice, straight spine," she used to say. "Please use it."

He stared at the pink bubbles in his shake cup. He felt Chop studying him and looked up.

"What else is eating you, dawg?" Chop said. "I can tell there's more on your mind."

"It's gonna sound stupid—"

Chop was smiling. "Code, last week at lunch I heard Gannon saying he was learning to like *tofu* as much as steak—and lemongrass tea as much as root beer! You really think you can top that?"

Cody stirred his shake, recalling the nightmares that invaded his sleep almost every night. A hulking thug named Gabe Weitz standing at the foot of his bed laughing and brandishing a tire iron. Weitz lining up against him in football. Weitz popping up from the backseat of a car and choking him from behind.

Pork Chop pounded a thick fist on the table, rattling the silverware and jarring Cody from his thoughts. His smile was impatient. "Spill it, Code. And I don't mean your shake."

"It's Weitz, okay? I can't get the dude outta my head."

Pork Chop frowned. "Uh, Weitz is dead. Look, I know he put us through heck for almost a whole year—trying to beat us down, breaking into your house, trying to run you down in his Loser-Mobile. But all that is over. People don't survive encounters with big trucks. And I know you don't believe in ghosts, so what's the problem?"

Cody leaned forward, put his elbows on the table, and sandwiched his head between his hands. "It's just that I don't know where Weitz is—you know what I mean?"

Chop arched his eyebrows. "Uh, I can show you exactly where he is. Just follow me over to Grant Cemetery. You know, I've thought about going over there and taking a leak on his grave—"

"—Chop! Stop, okay?" Cody was surprised at the anger in his voice. "First of all, you just don't do that to someone's grave, you know? C'mon, you're better than that. And, second of all, I didn't mean that I don't know where his body is. I'm talkin' about his soul."

Chop waved a hand dismissively in front of his face. "That dude had no soul."

Cody looked his friend in the eyes. He hoped Chop could see the sincerity, the earnestness he felt. "Chop, *everybody* has a soul."

Chop appeared to be considering the statement. "Well," he began slowly, "look at it this way, then. I'm not sure I agree with you about the whole heaven and hell thing, but if there is a hell, Weitz's sorry soul is definitely there. In the Extra Hot and Smoky section. That's what he deserves."

Ah, Chop, Cody thought, *sometimes I think you're so close to understanding what's what, but other times it seems like where you're at and where truth is are a million miles away.*

Chop was studying him again. Cody had seen the same expression on his friend's face when the two of them watched game tapes: the intense eyes, the creased forehead, the tightly pursed lips. "You gotta agree with me," Chop said after about a minute of silence. "You gotta admit that if anybody ever earned himself an all-expense paid trip to Hades Acres, it's Gabe Weitz. Dawg, you should feel good about that. If Weitz is roasting his toes in the underworld, justice has been served."

Cody shook his head, slowly, sadly. "Chop—you just don't get it. If Weitz didn't get right with God before he died, that's sad. That's a tragedy."

Chop belched. "You gotta be trippin'. Are you forgetting that, a few minutes before he died, he was trying to turn you into 140 pounds of roadkill?"

Cody finished his milk shake with a shiver. He wasn't sure if it was the cold beverage or the recollection of what happened along Highway 6 a month ago that was responsible. Ever since that day, when Weitz had apparently tried to run him down, he couldn't avoid whipping his head around whenever he heard a vehicle approaching from behind. And he could never watch a fiery car crash on TV without picturing Weitz's old Nissan truck cartwheeling off the road.

"Code," Chop said, interrupting his thoughts again, "I'm still waitin' for an answer. Tell me that after Weitz wrecked and you ran for help that you didn't consider just leavin' him to bleed out in his truck."

Cody felt himself teetering on the edge of tears. He wasn't sure why. He took a deep breath before he answered. "Chop, I promise I never considered that. I did think it was weird that I was running like crazy down the road trying to find help for my archenemy. But I knew what I had to do—what God wanted me to do. But I wasn't most concerned about finding medical help. I was more worried if Weitz had heard me when I told him he should pray. That's what still haunts me. Did he call out to God before he staggered onto the highway and got killed? Did he ask for forgiveness?"

"Like I said," Pork Chop said coldly, "he didn't deserve forgiveness."

"None of us does, big dawg. That's why it's called *forgiveness*. That's why we plead with each other for it. If we were entitled to it, we wouldn't have to beg. We'd just take it for granted, like, I don't know—the air all around us—and breathe it in. But forgiveness is like an act of mercy. You can't say to somebody—especially God—'You owe me some forgiveness. Give it to me right now!' Does that make sense?"

Chop appeared to stare at something above Cody's head for a few moments. Then his head began to bob slowly. "I think I'm feelin' what you're saying."

Cody heard himself sigh. "That's good to hear."

"So you've forgiven Weitz, then? For everything?"

Cody heard skepticism in his friend's voice, but also curiosity. "I really have, Chop. I can honestly say I don't have any bad feelings for him. 'Malice,' that's the word Pastor Taylor uses. Malice is like—"

"I know what malice is," Pork Chop said dismissively. "I read more than *Vibe* and *Sports Illustrated*, you know. But I have just one more question about this forgiveness thing."

"Yeah?"

"Well, if you've forgiven Weitz, how come the dude is still haunting you?"

Cody laughed sadly. "That, big man, is the question of the century. When I get it figured out, I'll let you know. But we both might be in an old folks' home before that happens."

"Maybe," Chop said, finishing his shake with a long, wet slurp. "But enough about all this mess. We got round two of the play-offs in a couple days. Claxton Hills, up at their place this time. It's time to put another beat-down on those rich posers."

In his mind, Cody replayed a highlight reel of the violent collisions he had absorbed during the regular-season battle against Claxton. *Those didn't feel like poser hits to me,* he said to himself.

Mr. Porter, who had run errands while his son and Cody dined at Dairy Delight, dropped Cody off at his house. "I'm right proud of you, Cody Martin," he said, with a tip of his trucker's cap. Then he poked a thumb toward the backseat in Chop's direction. "You and this-un have really shown me something this football season."

"Just wait till Friday, Pops," Chop said. "We're gonna light up those Claxton Hills pretty boys."

Mr. Porter plucked a handkerchief out of a front jeans pocket and blew his nose in three short bursts. "Now don't get all cocky on me, Deke Porter. Don't let your mouth start writin' checks that the rest of your body can't cash!"

Cody laughed and swung shut the door of the Porter supercab pickup. "See you tomorrow, Chop. Thanks for the ride, Mr. Porter."

A note was taped to the TV screen. Cody's dad and Beth were in Colorado Springs "taking care of a few wedding things."

"I wonder why Beth stuck the note to the TV," he muttered. "I'm not watching any TV tonight. There's no football, college or pro, on Wednesday nights. Man, some people just don't have a clue."

He climbed the stairs to his bedroom, his quad muscles throbbing and aching with each step. He flung himself on his bed and grabbed the phone to check messages.

The only one was from Robyn Hart.

"Yo, Cody. First of all, congrats again on a rockin' game this past week! You were awesome! Hey—I know you might still be sore from the game and your practices, but I was wondering if you might want to run with me tomorrow morning. Six-thirty or so? I'm having trouble getting myself motivated. I need my sometimes running partner. And who knows—it might help you loosen up a bit. So call me, okay?"

Root canal. Eating cold sauerkraut. Going to the opera. Singing a solo in church. Wearing a suit and tie—

and stiff, pinchy dress shoes. Surprise essay tests. Cody began to list the things he'd rather endure than tumble out of bed on a frigid Colorado morning and try to run on legs that, right now, felt as if they were on loan from his arthritic Grandmother Martin.

He hit the third button on speed dial. He got Robyn's machine. "Hey, Hart," he said, trying to keep his voice even, relaxed. "Sure, I'll run with you tomorrow. I'll just jog by your house around six-thirty or so. The extra half mile will help me work out some of the kinks. See you then."

Cody returned the phone to its charger. *You're such a dork*, he told himself. *You just agreed to do something you totally don't want to do. To help a girl! What's wrong with you, anyway?*

He yawned and settled onto his bed, hoping he'd be able to enjoy a nightmare-free slumber. He tried to convince himself that the run with Robyn was no big deal. She had gone out for cross-country this past season, eventually working her way onto the JV team. But she had wanted to run with the varsity, and that didn't happen.

Cody was sure that hitting the roads in the mornings was helping her to ease the disappointment—as well as getting her in shape for basketball season and laying a solid foundation for track in the spring.

"I'm just doing a bud a solid," he whispered. "No big deal."

He smiled as he imagined Chop was in the room listening to him. *The big fella wouldn't believe any of what I just said*, he thought. *I'm not even sure I believe it.*

... and Hunted

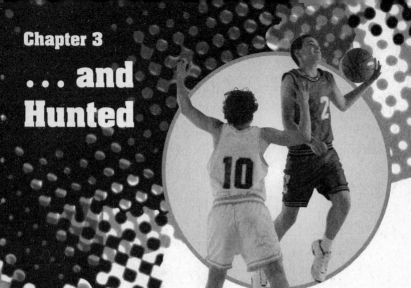

Ⅰt's nice of you to get up so early and run with me, *again*, Cody," Robyn said, her voice smooth despite the brisk pace she was setting. "Two days in a row. That's sweet of you."

Cody shrugged. "Just want to help a fellow athlete. Besides, we'll just do walk-throughs this afternoon at practice, and if I don't burn up at least some nervous energy, I won't be able to sleep tonight."

Robyn coughed softly, sending a round puff of vaporized air in front of her. "Anyway, if I'm going to make varsity track in the spring, I'm gonna need this extra work. I'm so bummed about cross-country this year.

Maybe I shoulda played volleyball. I just don't know. But, the main thing is, thanks for doing this with me."

Cody struggled a bit to keep up. His quadricep muscles ached with the deep-seated pain of yesterday's gassers—seven all-out sprints across the width of the football field. He gulped a lungful of air. "No problem. Glad to do it. It's not safe for a girl to be running alone on these mean streets."

Robyn giggled. "Yeah. Grant's streets are really mean. You never know when one of the chickens from the Hanson farm is going to escape and go looking for trouble."

"Or one of their cats," Cody offered.

"Ha. Those cats are so fat and lazy; the only way they could hurt you is if you tripped over one of them."

Cody laughed politely. He glanced at his watch, which read 7:21. "Time to head back to the school," he said, trying not to sound too eager. As they wheeled around and headed back down Main Street, he felt Robyn studying him. *I hope I don't have something hanging out of my nose,* he thought. *Or maybe I'm sweating too much.*

"Cody," she said finally, "is it still hard—dealing with your mom's death? I mean, it's been over a year, but I don't know if I could ever get past something like that. I hope you don't mind my asking.

But it's something I think about—pray about. Worry about you over."

Cody flashed her his Brave Smile. He was the master of the Brave Smile. He practiced it in his bathroom mirror almost every morning. "Let me put it this way, Hart. Every morning, I wake up wondering, 'Will this be the day when it finally stops hurting so much?' I'm still waiting."

Robyn dipped her head. "I'm so sorry."

Cody looked at her. She appeared to be on the verge of tears. *Can't have that happen*, he told himself. *If she starts crying, I might start too. That would be quite a sight—two frosh jocks running along Main Street sobbing like babies.*

"I am making progress though," he said quickly. "It's like, the pain's still there, but this weight that I've been feeling on my chest every morning is getting lighter. It used to be like a forty-five-pound weight plate, but lately it's been more like a thirty-five, maybe even a twenty-five."

Robyn laughed softly. "Leave it to a guy to put everything in weight-lifting terms."

They grew silent as they turned right off Main and headed to the high school. Cody noticed that his breaths were coming twice as fast as Robyn's. He wasn't sure if that was a sign that she was in much better shape than he was—or if the fact that he was running next to her, her ponytail swishing from side to side—had something to do with it.

They reached the bottom of Heartbreak Hill, the steep eighty-yard incline that crested near the main entrance to Grant High School. The hill had other names, especially among the athletes who had to sprint it as punishment for a poor game or a sloppy practice. But Cody didn't use any of those names, at least not in front of Robyn.

"Are you ready for Heartbreak?" Robyn asked.

"Oh, yeah," he replied grimly. "Always."

Robyn rose on her toes, swinging her arms. Cody lengthened his stride, feeling his quads rebel. *Just keep up with her*, he admonished himself. *Don't pass her, or she'll think you're challenging her. And the way your wheels are hurtin', you're not up to that kinda challenge. Think of the game tomorrow.*

He let her nudge ahead as they topped the hill.

"Good run, Cody," she said, extending her hand, palm up.

He froze for a moment. What to do about that hand: slap it, give it a squeeze? Or was it just a symbolic gesture, and he wasn't supposed to do anything? After an awkward pause, he grabbed her hand and shook it, just as he'd seen greeters do at church. *Ah, man*, he scolded himself, *I can't believe I just did that!*

Robyn giggled. "Nice to meet you too, Cody Martin, sir." That was followed by more giggling.

Cody started jogging backward. "I'm gonna run a bit more," he said, trying to sound casual. "Try to loosen up my legs. They're still a little tight."

Robyn just smiled. Cody turned and quickened his pace. "What my legs really are," he muttered to himself, "are dead. Just like my brain."

As a grade-schooler, Cody used to pretend he was being followed in the library, in the mall, even in church when he got to youth group early. His heart would start drumming as he ducked around corners or stutter-stepped his way downstairs. The imaginary chase always thrilled him, but it was a safe thrill.

Now he wished he had taken those fantasies more seriously—and paid closer attention during all the secret-agent movies he had seen before he gave them up in favor of sci-fi flicks. Because now he was certain that he was being followed through Cedar Heights Mall.

The guy tailing him was big, at least six three and well over two hundred pounds. He looked older than college age, maybe twenty-five. And he looked vaguely familiar, but Cody couldn't recall why. Perhaps he had attended Crossroads Community Church at some point. But if that were the case, he definitely had not sported a Death Metal T-shirt then. Pastor Taylor wouldn't have stood for that.

Cody threaded his way through the Thursday-night-at-the-mall traffic. He reached a long escalator at the south end of the mall's first level. He stepped carefully onto the moving steel steps and half turned so that he could monitor his stalker.

Mr. Death Metal walked head down toward the escalator. Cody swallowed hard. He almost stumbled as the escalator reached the second level. He made a sharp left turn and speed walked toward Pet Planet. He stepped through the entryway and the sharp smell—a mixture of pet food before and after digestion—filled his nostrils.

Through a glass display area that contained a half-dozen kittens romping amid shredded newspaper, he could see the escalator. Mr. Death Metal reached the top, took two steps forward, then stopped.

Why is he stopping? Cody wondered. *If he were going to a store, he'd just go there. This is* so not *good. Why did I listen to Beth?* "Come to the mall with your dad and me, Cody. It'll be fun. It'll take your mind off the big game tomorrow. Give you something to do besides sit in the house and obsess about Claxton Hills until you make yourself sick!"

Cody almost cried out when he realized the man had spotted him. Cody moved toward the back of the store past aquariums teeming with multicolored fish. When he reached a large metal tank housing three lethargic turtles, he stopped. The pet shop was narrow, with only three cramped aisles, like a miniature bowling alley. A guy could get cornered easily.

Mr. Death Metal was at the entrance now. He stopped for a moment to watch the kittens, then slid to his right and headed toward Cody.

God, he prayed, *I know that you know my favorite prayer. I probably don't even have to say it, but— HELP!*

Cody waited until his stalker was halfway down the aisle, then darted up the middle of the store. He didn't even risk a glance at Mr. Death Metal. Once outside Pet Planet, he turned left and sprinted. He could see heads turning to watch him. Two frowning mothers pulled their strollers out of his way.

They must think I'm a shoplifter—or a lunatic, he thought. *And I don't care.* He arrived at another escalator and sprinted up it, taking the moving steps two at a time.

Mr. Death Metal was still on his trail. The big man didn't run, but his stiff, brisk walk betrayed someone on a mission.

Cody waited at the top of the escalator. *Okay*, he told himself, *I have to do one thing, just to prove I'm not crazy paranoid.*

Mr. Death Metal stepped on the escalator. He walked up the steps until his path was blocked by a thin, white-haired man holding the hand of a pigtailed girl in a long, yellow dress.

Cody forced himself to stare at Mr. Death Metal's face. *Gotta make eye contact*, he told himself, *then I'll know if it's on.*

The man was halfway up the escalator now. Cody stepped forward, as if he were going to pull a Pork Chop stunt and try to descend against the flow. Mr. Death Metal met his stare and gave an exaggerated, palms-up shrug. As if to convey, "What's the use of running? You can't escape."

Cody stepped back. "Okay," he whispered to himself. "You wanted to know if it was on. Well, it's on."

He sprinted again. He passed a bookstore, an athletic shoe store, and an apparel shop for the Plus-Size Woman. The food court was just ahead. He could smell the appealing, mingling aromas of various fried foods. Between Nacho Loco and the Donut Factory was a long hallway leading to some restrooms. He whipped his head around. Mr. Death Metal wasn't in his sight line. He slowed to a walk to avoid colliding with a business executive exiting the men's room.

Inside the rearmost stall, Cody fought to slow his hungry, panting breaths. His T-shirt clung to his back, just as it did after a full-court basketball scrimmage. He locked the door and stood just in front of the toilet, facing forward.

He waited. Presently, the door hinges whined. *Is someone coming or going?* he wondered. Then he heard the telltale sound of footfalls on the sticky floor. Coming, was the answer. Right at him.

The footsteps stopped in front of Cody's stall. The door rattled as a hand pushed against it. Cody made his voice as low as a fourteen-year-old in the early stages of puberty could. "Occupied," he said flatly.

"That's okay," a voice answered. "I can wait."

Cody gulped. *Man, what I wouldn't give for a mall security dude who drank too much coffee at dinner.*

Cody scanned his memory trying to identify his stalker. *I'm pretty sure I've seen that face before, but it must have been a long, long time ago. Or maybe I'm just trying to convince myself I know this guy, because it would be even more terrifying to be attacked by a total stranger. And on the night before a play-off game, to boot! I'm gonna be a wreck tomorrow!*

The entrance door moaned again, and Cody heard two boisterous voices arguing over the previous weekend's Denver Broncos game. One guy's voice grew louder as he fought to be heard over the hissing of a sink faucet.

Okay, Cody resolved. *Time to exit. It stinks in here, and if Death Metal Dude is gonna kill me, he's gonna have to do it in front of witnesses!*

He drew in a deep breath and turned the latch. Mr. Death Metal turned his body slightly, but he didn't back up. Warily, Cody stepped by him. He locked his eyes on the exit. One of the Broncos fans was furiously rubbing his hands together under an air dryer. The other was studying his reflection in a mirror.

If I run, Cody wondered, *what will happen? Will one of those guys grab me, or will they let me go by? Maybe they'll slow down Death Metal Dude if he sprints after me.*

The sound of a clearing throat yanked Cody from his thoughts. "Cody Martin," the man in the Death Metal shirt said evenly. "We need to talk. I'm Gary Weitz. Gabe Weitz's big brother."

Cody felt fear envelop him like a fog. *So that's where I've seen that face before. Gary's face isn't as fat as his brother's, but those cold eyes—there's definitely a family resemblance.*

One of the Broncos fans shoved the other out the door, leaving Cody alone with a guy whose shirt proclaimed "Death."

"What do you want with me?" Cody was surprised at the anger in his voice. He had meant to sound meek, sympathetic.

"Like I said," Gary Weitz explained, his tone still eerily calm, "we need to talk."

"Look," Cody said, "my dad is here at the mall and I was supposed to meet up with him a while ago. He's going to be looking for me."

Weitz smiled. "This won't take long."

Cody swallowed what little saliva remained in his mouth. "Those guys who were in here—they saw us. They saw your face. If anything happens—"

The smile again. "I don't care what they saw. It doesn't matter."

Cody willed himself to look into those cold eyes. "I'm not afraid of you," he said. *Helpful hint*, he scolded himself, *next time you tell someone you're not afraid of him, try to do it without your voice shaking.*

"I think you are afraid," Weitz said. "You're sweating."

"I'm sweating because you chased me all over the whole stinkin' mall."

"Yeah, but athlete sweat and fear sweat have distinct aromas. You're a jock. You should know that. And I smell fear."

Just keep talking, big man, Cody thought. *The longer we talk, the better the chances someone else will come in. Maybe even Dad.*

But Weitz was reaching for him. Cody stepped back, banging into the stall door. "Cody," Weitz said. "I'm not going to hurt you."

Cody cocked his head and narrowed his eyes suspiciously. "Yeah? You mighta told me that right up front, then."

Another smile. "I have to admit—I was enjoying watching you squirm. See, sometimes I find myself wanting to blame you for what happened."

"You gotta be kidding me!" Again, Cody's own anger shocked him. "Your brother attacked me, and that's what started the whole thing. I don't know what he told you, but all I did was let a door close behind me one time after basketball practice. And for that, he goes Extreme Wrestling on me and slams me into the door, then tosses me in the snow. Later on, he chucks beer bottles at me and Pork Chop, then chases me and another one of my friends, and, finally, tries to run me down with his truck! I never talked trash to him. Never flipped him off. Nothing. Look, I am sorry about what happened to your brother. But what happened— that's on him, not me."

Weitz dipped his head. "I know."

Cody felt his head shaking in bewilderment. "Then why did you come after me?"

"I wasn't coming after you, not like you're thinking. I just need to tell you something. And ask you one question." Weitz's arms were folded defiantly across his chest. He let them drop to his sides.

"I'm listening," Cody said.

Weitz cleared his throat. "Gabe wasn't trying to run you down," he said. "Not really."

"He coulda fooled me!"

The elder Weitz sighed wearily. "He was just trying to scare you. Look, he was my brother, and I know he had a mean streak. It's kinda my fault, I think. I picked on him, harassed him all his life. Anyway, he mentioned you from time to time. I think he really hated you at one point, because Pork Chop's brother, Doug, humiliated him with that one-punch KO. And that all kinda started with you—even though I know it wasn't your fault or anything. But after a while, he got over wanting to hurt you. He just wanted to throw a scare into you occasionally. It became kinda like a hobby."

Cody crossed his arms. "Collecting stamps—*that's* a hobby. Stalking someone doesn't seem like just a hobby to me. It's more like an obsession."

"Really? Then why did you tell the police that you thought the whole truck thing was probably an accident—or a prank gone bad?"

Cody felt the question pressing in on him. He recalled the police interview—and reinterview. "I'm not sure if I know the answer to that," he began. "I mean, your brother was *killed*, after all. Whether he was attacking me or just trying to scare me, he paid the steepest price. I didn't see what good accusing him of attempted murder would do. And, besides, I wasn't sure. And I don't go around throwing serious accusations like that unless I'm 100 percent sure. You know, back in Old Testament times, if you accused someone of a crime punishable by death, you had to be willing to participate in the execution yourself."

Weitz raised his eyebrows. "I didn't know that."

Cody sensed he was out of danger. Still, he wanted to escape from the restroom. Gary Weitz seemed like a reasonable guy, but he *was* Gabe Weitz's brother, and the momentum could shift suddenly—just as it did in sports.

"Uh, Gary," Cody said, "you mentioned that you had a question?"

Weitz nodded. "Yeah. Well, if I understand correctly what happened, you had gone for help when Gabe stumbled out of his truck and onto that old highway."

"That's right. I really did all I could to get help to him as soon as I could. I ran as hard as I could to find someone."

Weitz's voice was little more than a whisper. "I believe you. What I'm wondering is, you must have known he was alive if you went for help. So, did you talk to him or anything? Did he say anything to you?"

Cody shook his head sadly. "No. I don't know if he was conscious. But I did talk to him. I tried to assure him that I was going for help. And I told him I would pray for him. I told him he should pray too."

Weitz looked at Cody. His eyes glistened. "I hope he did."

"I do too," Cody said quietly.

Weitz looked up at the ceiling. "You know, at his funeral, a few of his buddies were there. At the cemetery, before they put my brother in the ground, these guys walked by his casket and poured beer on it. Some ritual, huh?"

Cody nodded slowly.

"I mean," Weitz said, his voice quaking slightly, "is that what it comes down to? Is that what a guy's life stands for? Your best friends march stone-faced by your dead body and pour beer on you?"

Cody searched every corner of his brain for a response. All he could find was, "I'm sorry."

Weitz took two steps backward. "Well, you better go find your dad."

Cody walked purposefully toward the door.

"Thanks for what you did, Cody," he heard Weitz call behind him. He turned and nodded.

Chapter 4

Postseason Blues

Claxton Hills High School was surrounded by ranch-style homes framed by evergreen trees, rose bushes, and hedges manicured with surgical precision. It was a private school where parents coughed up more than $8,000 a year to protect their kids from the dangers—both real and perceived—of South Denver's public schools.

As Cody, with his Eagle teammates, traipsed through the gymnasium, he noted the many banners adorning all four walls. Conference, district, and state titles in almost every sport—gymnastics, cross-country, track, baseball, soccer. He didn't notice any football banners, but he knew Claxton Hills hoped to remedy that short-coming—and this evening's game was part of the quest. Grant, which finished the regular season at 5–3, had handed the Lancers their only loss of the season, so Claxton entered the play-offs as a higher seed—a vengeful higher seed.

When the Eagles were taped up and dressed out, Coach Morgan called them to the center of the visitors' locker room. As he began to speak, ATV and Clark began to tap their helmets, gently and rhythmically, on the benches where they sat. Coach Morgan raised his voice slightly, and the cadence of his speech changed, keeping rhythm with his two star players' percussion backdrop. Soon, other Eagles joined their leaders. Some began clacking their cleats against the concrete floor. Something about the aura reminded Cody of church.

"Forty-eight minutes," the coach was saying. "Maximum effort on every play. Play with courage. Play with pride. Play with intensity. You are Eagles! It's time to fly high!"

The tapping and banging and pounding accelerated steadily until it sounded to Cody like a violent hailstorm.

ATV stood, threw back his head and bellowed a primal war cry. Others joined in. Coach Morgan waited for the frenzy to subside. "Let's take a minute," he said. Almost in unison, the team dropped to one knee.

Cody closed his eyes tightly. *Any glory, Lord, that comes from this game*, he prayed earnestly, *let it be yours. No one else's.*

He opened his eyes. Clark's hands were folded in front of him, his lips moving slightly. Pork Chop stared straight ahead, drinking in huge gulps of air. Phillips crossed himself before standing quietly and sliding his helmet over his head.

Coach Morgan waited for all of his players to stand. "Let's bring it in, fellas," he called. The team formed a massive huddle in the middle of the locker room, all extending arms toward the center, making a huge stack of their hands. "Let's hear 'team' on three," he commanded.

Cody yelled the word as loud as he could, but he couldn't hear his own voice amid the deeper, louder ones surrounding him.

Cody followed his teammates on the field, which was lit up like a birthday cake. Throughout pregame warm-ups, Cody had to constantly battle the urge to stop and stare in wonder at the scene around him. "There must be 250 kids just in the Claxton band," he mumbled. "It's a good thing this stadium is so big, because it looks like the whole city of Denver is here!"

The much smaller visitors' stands were full too, but the size contrast between the Eagle and Lancer faithful reminded Cody of Gideon and the Midianites.

ATV gave the visiting fans cause to cheer early in the game, booting the opening kickoff five yards beyond the end zone, then sacking Eric Faust, the Lancers' college-bound QB, on first down.

But it was a long time before the Grant High parents, alumni, and fans found cause to cheer again. In the meantime, Eagle defensive stalwart Jeff "Truck" Tucker broke his ankle midway into the first quarter. ATV began to suffer from back spasms a few minutes later. By late in the second quarter, he couldn't move without crying out in pain and frustration.

Finally, with thirty-eight seconds remaining in the half, Clark body-slammed Faust in his own end zone for a safety. But that cut only slightly into Claxton Hills' 14–0 lead.

Cody found himself in the thick of the first-half action as Faust relied heavily on his two talented wide receivers, the stocky and tough Sam Butler and lanky and fleet Hayden Owens-Tharpe. Working mostly against Butler, Cody enjoyed success early in the game, as he crowded Butler at the line of scrimmage, preventing him from getting into his routes. However, on the Lancers' final drive of the first quarter, Cody bit on an out-and-up route and had to grab Butler's jersey to keep him from getting open for a long bomb from Faust. The resulting holding penalty was key in the Lancers getting on the scoreboard first.

On the next Claxton Hills possession, Cody found himself with a clear path to Faust on a corner blitz, but the QB ducked under the attempted sack, then scooted around the right end for twenty-nine yards.

As a result, Cody spent the early portion of halftime in the rear of the locker room muttering to himself. He startled when he realized Coach Morgan was standing right behind him.

"Martin," the coach said, his voice little more than a rasp, "get yourself under control. Get your focus on the second half, understand?"

Cody swallowed hard. "Yes, Coach, it's just that—"

Coach Morgan shook his head. "I don't wanna hear it. All things considered, you did okay. I can't fault your effort. And I'd rather have a holding penalty then give Butler a free pass to the end zone. So just keep playing the game. You're a freshman playing varsity football. I'm not expecting you to set the world on fire. Just play hard every down."

The Eagles moved into field goal range early in the third quarter, but with ATV barely able to move, much less kick, they had to go for it on fourth and eight from the Lancer twenty-five. Hammond, the Grant QB, picked up only six yards on a draw play, and the Eagles turned the ball over on downs.

Claxton Hills got a bonus on the change of posses-
sion when Pork Chop was flagged for unsportsman-
like conduct after the play. The Eagle left tackle and
the Lancer right defensive end began shoving each
other long after the referees had whistled the play dead.
The pushing match escalated when Chop grabbed his
opponent by the face mask and flung him to the
ground.

Chop appeared ready to pounce when Clark and
Hammond intervened and dragged him—amid bellows
of protest—off the field.

I gotta get over to him, Cody told himself as Pork
Chop reached the sideline. *Gotta get him calmed down
or he's gonna get tossed out of the game.*

But by the time Cody arrived at his friend's side,
Chop was quiet, sullen. "Chop," Cody said, tentatively,
"you okay? What was that all about?"

"He said 'the word' to me," Chop muttered.
"Dropped the N-bomb. I'm not gonna take that."

Cody felt anger rising inside him but quickly
pushed it down. His friend needed a calming influence
right now. "Look, big dawg," he said, "for someone to
say that to you—that's just wrong. But you gotta keep
your head in the game. We're only down twelve
points. But with Truck and ATV hurting, we need you
more than ever."

"It doesn't matter anyway," Chop said robotically. "It's over."

Cody felt his jaw drop. "I can't believe I'm hearing this from you! We've got almost half a game ahead of us. Over? No way is this over!"

It *was* over.

With a two-touchdown lead, Claxton Hills abandoned its passing game and kept the ball on the ground. With Tucker and ATV missing from the defense, Grant couldn't keep the first-down chains from moving. Clark was flying all over the field, on his way to a twenty-six-tackle performance, but he couldn't be everywhere. The Lancers moved into field goal range twice, connecting on one of the two opportunities.

Trailing 17–2 with only nine minutes to play, the Grant coaches grew desperate and inserted Clark into the offense, as tailback. "We gotta have our best player involved in every possible play," Cody heard Coach Morgan say to a nodding Coach Curtis.

After three straight four-yard runs up the gut, Clark faked toward the middle of the line, then bounced outside. He outsprinted everyone to the end zone. Claxton Hills—17, Grant—8.

Hammond, ATV's replacement at kicker, somehow slipped the extra-point try *under* the crossbar, meaning Grant couldn't tie the game with another touchdown, followed by a two-point conversion. The Eagles had to produce two scores in just over seven minutes. And that was only if they could keep Claxton Hills off the scoreboard.

The Lancers didn't score again, but it didn't matter. Faust led his team on a sixty-eight-yard drive that stalled at the Grant twenty. Claxton's kicker shanked a field goal attempt, but Grant got the ball back with just over two minutes remaining.

The game ended a few plays later, with Brendan Clark dragging half the opposing defense across midfield. Even most of the Claxton faithful gave him a standing ovation when Hammond and Phillips helped the exhausted Eagle to his feet.

Then the Claxton fans left the stands and poured onto the field. Cody stood on the sidelines and watched the throng bobbing up and down. Occasionally, a hat, a scarf, or even a shoe, flew up from the celebration.

The Claxton Hills public address announcer proclaimed that he had "a very important reminder," but as he delivered the message, his voice became progressively shriller, faster, and more distorted until all Cody could decipher was the occasional "future state champion Lancers!"

He looked around for Pork Chop who, at one point in the fourth quarter, had shared his plan to track down the Claxton defensive end and renew their grudge match. Cody said a silent prayer of thanks when he saw Chop standing alone on the all-weather track that circled the field.

"Check that out, Chop," he said, pointing to the celebration still buzzing on the field. "Think that'll be us someday?"

"No," Chop said flatly.

Cody rolled his eyes. "C'mon, big man. I know it hurts to lose. But we have three more seasons to get where those guys are now."

Chop turned to him, eyes narrowed. "I can count, Code. But *we* aren't ever going to be out there like that."

Cody stepped back, rocked by the force, the certainty, of his friend's proclamation. "How can you say that?" he asked.

"Because," came the answer, "I'm moving away. Far away."

Chapter 5
Pulled Apart

It's been a long time since we've done this," Blake Randall said, settling into a chair behind his desk. "That might be a good sign—maybe you're not having as many life challenges right now. But I have to say, with everything that's going on in your life, that's a little hard to believe."

Cody exhaled slowly. "Yeah. I know it's all a bit much for me to deal with. I mean, Chop moving away? That's like taking a baseball bat to the stomach. And the wedding at the end of the week? Well, that's kinda like—being hunted down by a pack of wolves or something. You keep running, but you know, eventually, they're going to catch you."

Cody, sitting on a metal folding chair facing Blake's desk, realized he had been directing his words to the infamously ugly carpet in his youth pastor's office. He lifted his head. Blake was nodding slowly, giving him that familiar understanding smile.

"It's amazing, Cody, the changes life throws at us sometimes. It seems like things happen that will overwhelm us, even ruin our lives."

Cody rested his elbows on his knees, then let his chin drop into his hands. "Having Pork Chop as my best friend for all these years has been a gift from God; I have no doubt about that. I don't know how I would have survived my mom's death without him. And he's helped with this whole marriage thing too. Even though I still hate that it's going to happen—when he makes jokes about it and stuff—that helps me keep it in perspective, I guess."

"He's a good friend, Cody. No doubt about it. You're blessed."

"I *was* blessed," Cody corrected Blake.

Blake was waving his forefinger from side to side. "That's not true. Don't discount all of the years you've been best friends. And don't think it's over just because he *might* move. You said yourself it's not definite. Besides, Tennessee isn't the end of the world, you know. You have the phone. You have email. Pretty soon you'll have a driver's license. Maybe we'll take a road trip someday."

"Maybe," Cody muttered.

Blake cleared his throat. "Well, enough about that for now. Let's talk about the wedding."

Cody stood suddenly. "You know what? Let's not. I just don't think I can talk about that right now, B. It kills me every time I think about it. Look, I know changes happen in life. I'm just not ready for *this* change." He turned for the door. He expected Blake to jump up and try to stop him. Instead, he heard only a brief, muttered sentence. He wheeled to face Blake again.

"Did you say something?"

"Not to you."

Cody cocked his head. "Uh, there's no one else in the room. Unless you're keeping a hamster in your desk drawer or something."

Blake smiled. "You're forgetting someone."

Cody returned the smile with a sheepish one of his own. "So you were praying—about what? That I'd grow up and quit being so selfish? That I'd quit mopin' around?"

"Nah, Code. I just prayed a verse for you."

"You gonna recite it for me?"

"I don't think so. It's Numbers 6, verses 24 through 26. Why don't you go look it up when you get home."

Cody tapped a forefinger on his bottom lip. "Numbers? I don't think I know any cool verses from Numbers."

Blake stood. His eyes met Cody's. "You will soon."

Cody sat on his bed flipping through the Old Testament. "Numbers, huh?" he said. "I thought that book just had a bunch of laws and genealogies and stuff. Or maybe I'm thinking of Leviticus."

He made it all the way to Ruth before he realized he had gone too far. He backtracked and finally found the verses: "The LORD bless you and keep you; the LORD make his face shine upon you and be gracious to you; the LORD turn his face toward you and give you peace." The words rang familiar. Pastor Taylor occasionally closed his sermons with them. *I never knew that prayer was right out of the Bible,* Cody thought. *I thought it was from one of those pastor's manuals or something.*

The screaming snapped Cody from his thoughts. Beth's voice was loud and shrill. "You're a big, foolish man!" she said. Or was it, "You're a pig—and a clueless man"?

Cody opened his door quietly. His dad was retorting now. "You were shamelessly flirting with our waiter all night. He must have thought I was your father."

"I was just being friendly," Beth spat back. "For Pete's sake, the guy looked about nineteen years old!"

"Closer to your age than I am."

He has a point there, Cody thought.

"Oh, so that's what this is all about. Your petty insecurity about your age. Look, Luke, I know you're forty-two. I can do the math. When I'm the age you are now, you'll be almost sixty. I understand that. I can live with that. The question is, can you?"

Cody leaned his head out of his doorway. *Don't want to miss Dad's response to this. That's one tough question.*

But no answer came.

Cody heard footsteps clicking across the hardwood floor toward the front door. He heard the door open. "Well," Beth said, sobbing now, "if you figure it out, call me. Preferably within the next three days, because I'm supposed to be getting married after that!" The door slam that followed was strong enough to knock something to the floor. *Probably one of Mom's Scripture plaques*, Cody reasoned. *Hope it's not the one that says "Blessed Are the Peacemakers."*

He slipped downstairs. His dad was pacing the living room. It reminded him of how Coach Curtis prowled the sidelines. Anxious. Nervous. Frustrated.

"Dad," he said softly, "you all right?"

His father turned to him. At first there was fire in his pale blue eyes, but just as Cody prepared himself for an angry lecture, the fire died. "I'm sorry, Cody," his dad sighed. "I know we must have upset you. Please forgive me. Us. I'm sure this is all rather shocking to you. You know, your mother and I rarely got into this kind of fight. The yelling, the slamming doors."

Cody tried to force a smile. "Dad, I've been playing sports for some short-tempered coaches for years and years. I've heard plenty of yelling. A little more isn't going to traumatize me or anything."

Cody's dad leaned against the front door. He appeared to be on the verge of sliding down to the floor. "I just don't know if I can take it, son. Beth is young and attractive. I'm neither young nor attractive. Then, tonight, she goes and flirts with this waiter, with his wrinkle-free face and dark black hair."

"She was really flirting with him, Dad? Like, what was she doing?"

"Well, she kept calling him 'homeboy' and smiling like she was doing a toothpaste commercial."

Cody let his gaze drop to the floor. It *was* the ceramic Peacemakers plaque that had fallen, he noted. It had split into two almost equal pieces, right between the lines that said "Blessed Are" and "the Peacemakers."

Cody closed his eyes and uttered a brief, silent prayer. *Well, it's not exactly stone tablets brought down from a mountaintop, but I get the message, Lord. Thanks.*

He took two steps toward the front door. "Uh, Dad," he began, "Beth calls *me* 'homeboy' sometimes. She says it to Chop, too. Maybe she doesn't mean anything by it. Maybe it's just a word."

Cody saw his dad straighten his stance a bit. "Perhaps," he mumbled. "But there was more to it than that, Cody. You should have seen the way she was smiling at him."

I can't believe I'm gonna say what I'm about to say, Cody marveled to himself. *Either I'm finally maturing a little bit—or I'm completely crazy.*

He cleared his throat. "Dad—Beth kinda smiles at everybody. I think she's just a friendly person. I've seen her smile at waiters and concession workers and ticket tearers at the movies and stuff. But she doesn't smile at them the way she smiles at you."

Cody saw genuine surprise flicker in his father's eyes. He wondered how long it had been since he'd seen that particular emotion. "Really, Cody? You're not saying this just to make me feel better?"

"It's true, Dad. Really." He drew in a long, deep breath. "Anyway, I think I'm gonna go back to my room now. I have some reading to do for school. And I need to start reviewing some basketball stuff Coach

Clayton gave me. Got to start thinking hoops now that football season is finally over."

Cody turned and slowly climbed the stairs. He heard his dad pick up the phone. "Beth," he said, "please don't hang up. I need to apologize."

Cody entered his room and flung himself on his bed. "Well, God," he whispered, "I think I did okay at being a peacemaker. Just like the plaque says. But I have to say, I don't see how I'm gonna be *blessed* by any of this."

The next morning was Thursday, the day Cody and Pork Chop planned to start basketball practice. Coach Clayton had been understanding about two of his key players being needed on the football team. But now that the Eagle gridders' play-off run was over, he was eager to shore up his squad. And Cody and Pork Chop had been key to the Grant hoopsters coming within an eyelash of the district championship as eighth graders.

Coach Clayton had tracked down Cody and Chop in the lunch room on the Monday following the loss to Claxton Hills, plopping down across from them.

"Hello, men," he had said, folding his long legs under the table. "I'm sorry the season's over, but you guys had a fine year. You should be proud of yourselves."

"I guess so," Chop replied, without looking up.

"It's hard to believe the season is really over," Cody added, trying to inject at least a little life into his voice.

Coach Clayton nodded. "So, how you guys feelin'? A bit sore, I would imagine."

"You would imagine correctly," Chop said, his voice still sullen.

"I don't take the kind of beating Chop does," Cody offered, "but I am banged up. Even my bruises have bruises!"

"Well," the coach said, extricating himself from the table and standing, "I know you might need to take two or three days off, but we're hurtin', fellas. Mr. Alston is running with the varsity. He'll probably be the second guy off the bench for them. And Terrance Dylan will start for the JV team. So—"

"How about Thursday, Coach?" Cody suggested. "That'll give us a few days to recoup. Get over the loss to Claxton. Heal up, you know?"

"I guess I can live with that, fellas. But if you start getting your legs under you before that, you know your way to the gym."

Pork Chop reported to practice on Tuesday, without telling Cody. So when Cody showed up Thursday morning, he was surprised to see his friend already in his practice jersey working with Coach Clayton on rebounding position.

"What's up, Chop?" he said, jogging toward them. "You camp out here last night? I can't remember the last time you beat me to practice—in any sport."

Cody saw Coach Clayton exchange glances with Chop, then jog toward Gannon, shouting, "Aw, for the love of David Thompson, Gannon! Can't you *try* to get some elevation on your jumper?"

"Dawg," Chop said, his voice just above a whisper, "I decided to start practicing a couple days ago."

The news almost caused Cody to step backward. "Uh, thanks for telling me. I woulda started with you, you know."

"Sorry. But I kinda decided I might as well get used to it, you know?"

Cody picked up a basketball that had rolled to a stop near his feet. He fired a hard chest pass to Chop. "Get used to what?" he asked accusingly.

Chop returned the pass, so softly that Cody had to stoop to catch it, near his ankles. "Don't front, Cody," he said sadly. "You know what I'm talking about. It's almost for sure that Dad's gonna sell the farm. He's getting older. Money's getting tighter. And with Doug up at college, the work load is puttin' a big hurt on both of us. You understand, right?"

Cody turned away, afraid that if he looked at Chop's pained face for one more second, he'd start to cry.

"There are about a thousand things I don't understand right now, Chop," he said as he trudged away. "I'll just add this to the list."

Friday after practice, Cody accepted a ride home from Pork Chop and his dad. As Cody slid out of the Porters' pickup, Chop held out his fist. "Get good rest tonight, dawg. You wanna be sharp for the wedding tomorrow. Don't want to see you fainting and doin' a face plant into the front pew." The words were vintage Pork Chop, but there was no genuine humor behind them. It was as if his friend were reading them for the first time from a script.

Cody smacked his knuckles against his friend's. "Yeah, you too. Don't want you falling asleep during the ceremony."

"Just think, Code, we don't have enough practices to play this weekend, but next weekend we'll be suiting up and playing hoops again. After playing varsity football, frosh hoops will be too easy. I bet we run the table—go undefeated!"

Mr. Porter chuckled. "You best focus on the business at hand: your *first* game of the season, next week. You're talkin' about chickens that ain't hatched yet. Now, quit your jawin' and let young Mr. Martin get inside. He's got a rehearsal dinner to get to."

Cody was standing in front of the refrigerator weighing his pre-dinner snack options when he heard the doorbell. Somehow, he knew it would be Beth.

"Hi," he said, summoning all the cheer he could muster and injecting it into his voice. "Come on in. Dad's not home yet. Probably still at work."

"Actually," she said, stepping across the threshold and into the living room, "he's already over at the church. I'm your ride tonight. Because, Cody, I want to talk to you. I'm not interrupting you, am I?"

"Nah," Cody said, taking a seat at the far end of the living room couch. Beth sat down at the other end, rotating her torso so that she faced him.

"I've been meaning to call you, but I thought a personal visit was more appropriate," she began.

Cody felt his heart accelerating. *I wonder what this is about*, he thought. *I mean, the wedding is back on, but maybe something's changed.*

Beth's voice was quiet, more subdued than usual. "Cody," she continued, "Luke—uh, I mean, your dad, told me how you sort of stood up for me over the whole alleged flirtation thing."

"Yeah?" Cody said, hoping Beth wouldn't note the suspicion in his voice.

"Well, I just want to thank you. Look, I know that you are not exactly thrilled about my marrying your dad tomorrow. So I know it took a lot of courage and integrity to do what you did. I mean, that could have been the thing that killed our plans—or at least put them on hold for a while. I'm not sure how you found it in yourself to defend me, but I'm so thankful you did. I'm blown away, in fact. I should have thanked you sooner, but—"

Cody got the sense that Beth was struggling to hold back tears. "I really can't take credit for what I did," he explained. "It was a God thing. He showed me what I needed to do. My part was just to obey."

Beth nodded. "I'm thankful you did. It means a lot. Look, I'm not going to give you a big speech or anything, because I'm sure you have so much on your mind and heart already. But I'll just say this: All I'm asking for is a chance. I care about you. We'll find a way to make this work. Okay?"

"Okay," Cody whispered.

"You know, I love you."

The words froze in Cody's brain. *Some people say I love you just like tossing you a ball during a game of catch*, he thought. *They expect you to toss the words right back. Like a reflex or something. It's not fair. If you don't say it back, it's like taking somebody else's ball and walking home with it.*

He felt the scrutiny of Beth's gaze on him. "Uh—" he began.

She smiled reassuringly. "You don't have to say anything back, homeboy. I don't want you to say it until you mean it. But I hope that day will come sometime."

Cody nodded.

"And you don't have to call me Mom or anything like that. You call me whatever you want—well, within reason anyway."

Cody forced a laugh. "Well, you always call me homeboy, maybe you should be homegirl."

"You think your dad will go for that? He might think it's kinda informal."

Cody laughed, not forcing it this time. "Dad could stand to be a lot more informal."

"Amen to that," Beth said, standing. "You start getting your game face on, okay? Best man—that's a heavy responsibility, homeboy."

"Thanks, Beth—I mean, *homegirl!*"

Cody finally decided on two Pop-Tarts as a snack. Then he was able to squeeze in almost a whole quarter of the Lakers and the Pistons while Beth dressed for the rehearsal dinner.

After returning home from the dinner, Cody would have sprinted up the stairs to his room had he not feared leaving much of said dinner on the stairs. "I never shoulda had that second steak," he groaned. "What was I thinking?"

He changed out of his pants and into his baggiest sweats, then eased himself onto his bed. He checked the phone messages. Pastor Taylor, Pork Chop, Blake, Doug Porter, and Robyn had all left words of encouragement for him. He deleted all but Robyn's, which said, "Cody, you are so awesome. I'm proud of you. Who would have thought you'd make it into the thick of varsity football play-offs as a frosh? And I know you're gonna have a rockin' basketball season too. And as for tomorrow, all I can say is that you're being very mature about everything—even though I know you must feel so torn up inside. Anyway, just know I'll be thinking of you tomorrow. God bless."

Cody opened his blinds so that he could see the bluish glow of a three-quarter moon. "Dear God," he prayed, "I've never had so much uncertainty in my life. My family life is about to change forever. My best friend might move away. I'm in wa-aa-ay over my head trying to transition from football to basketball. I'm so tired. So sore. And, Robyn, that's another mystery. Are we getting to be more than friends? And is that a good thing or a bad thing? It's like, there's nothing I can be sure of; nothing I can hang onto. Except you. In this mixed up life of mine, thanks for always being there for me. Amen."

Cody shot a glance at Becky, Beth's sister. She nodded, curled her left hand around the crook of his elbow, and the two of them walked in perfect synchronicity down the middle aisle of Crossroads Community Church.

When they arrived at the front of the church, they parted ways, and Cody took his place next to Ray Fairchild, one of his dad's work friends. Cody scanned the congregation, allowing himself a small smile when he spotted Pork Chop, flanked by his father and big brother, about halfway back.

Chop, exaggerating every move, straightened his tie, then smoothed both eyebrows with thick fingers. Then he nodded at Cody. This last gesture, Cody knew, was sincere, not just for show.

Cody closed his eyes. *Okay, God. It's really going to happen, isn't it? Please help me do my part to make this day happy for Dad and Beth. Forgive me for being selfish. Amen.*

Cody almost added a P.S. to his prayer, noting that there was still time for things to be postponed. A power failure or a small earthquake wouldn't be the worst thing in the world, would it?

Then he saw his dad and Pastor Taylor emerge from a side door near the front of the church. *Chop was right*, he thought. *That's the face of a genuinely happy man.*

Cody extended his hand as his father took his place beside him. Luke ignored the hand and embraced his son with both arms.

"Oh, sweet!" Cody heard someone in the congregation gush.

Cody straightened his sports jacket. The church organ swelled as Mrs. Leadbetter launched into the "Wedding March."

Beth stepped gracefully down the aisle accompanied by her father, a red-faced man built like a fire hydrant. *If he played football*, Cody figured, *he'd have been a center, maybe a guard. And if baseball was his game? A catcher. Definitely a catcher.*

As the ceremony continued, Cody scanned the congregation noting how many people dabbed at their eyes with handkerchiefs and tissues. He knew that Pastor Taylor was delivering another of his famously poignant wedding messages, but he couldn't concentrate on the words.

The only words he could focus on were the ones that flashed in his brain, like the neon sign over the Dairy Delight: DON'T FAINT, DON'T CRY, DON'T FAINT, DON'T CRY.

Fail to heed either of these warnings, Cody knew, and his father's wedding day could be ruined.

Cody's narrow train of thought derailed momentarily when the pastor got to the part about "You got a problem with this marriage? Then speak now, or forever hold your peace."

Okay, Cody tried to send a telepathic message to the congregants, *here's your last chance, people. C'mon, somebody out there must have an objection—what are you waiting for?*

But no objections were forthcoming. Cody stifled a sigh and handed his sniffling father the ring. *Okay, Lord*, he prayed. *I get the message. Your will, not Cody Martin's, be done. But I hope it wasn't too bad a thing to hold out one last little hope—*

Cody cut his prayer short as he fumbled the handoff of the ring. It dropped toward the ground. Cody could imagine it hitting the floor and rolling into a heating vent, where it would be lost forever. Instinctively, he bent his knees and shot out his right hand, quick as a rattlesnake strike. Relief warmed him as his fist clenched around the ring.

His father winked at him. "Nice catch," he whispered.

The reception was held in the church's fellowship area. Cody was hugged and patted by dozens of people, many of whom he didn't know. *This is kinda like being in the locker room after a big game,* he thought. *Except for all the perfume and cologne. And thank goodness I don't have to see any of these people naked, especially old Mrs. Leadbetter. Yuck!*

He had just been sandwiched between two large women wearing blood-red hats, describing themselves as "your new aunties!" when he saw Blake approaching.

The youth pastor smiled widely at the women, announcing, "I need to steal this young man from you for a moment if I may, ladies."

Giggling, they released Cody from between them.

"They're getting ready to cut the cake," Blake offered.

"Oh, goodie," said the woman with the slightly bigger and redder hat. "I just adore wedding cake!"

"Thanks for the rescue, B," Cody whispered, as he followed Blake up the stairs and into the youth pastor's office.

Blake sat on his desk, rather than behind it, and gestured for Cody to sit down facing him.

"I wish you could see your face right now, Cody," the youth pastor began. "There must be a whirlwind going on inside your head. Want to take a shot at trying to explain to me what's going on up there? I'm concerned about you."

"I'm not sure if I can put it into words, B. It's kinda like eating a really good meal, and that makes you happy, right? But, then, something about the meal doesn't sit quite right in your stomach. Maybe it was too sweet or too rich. Or maybe you ate too much. And, all of the sudden, you think you're gonna puke. That's how I feel, I guess. Does that make any sense?"

Blake pursed his lips and nodded slowly. "You know, Code, it does. It ain't poetry, but I think I see what you're getting at. You're happy for your dad. Maybe for Beth too. But on the other hand—"

"Yeah—the other hand. The one that just balled itself into a fist and drilled me in the stomach." Cody stood. "I think I'm gonna go outside and walk around for a while. Get some air."

"Where are you planning to go?"

Cody tried to smile, but he got the feeling the attempt wasn't successful. "Anyplace some perfumed women with scary red hats won't try to hug me."

"Hey, dude," Blake called after Cody, as he started to walk away, "you want me to grab you a piece of cake?"

Cody turned around. "Nah, man. You know, for the first time in my whole life, I'm not hungry for cake."

Chapter 6

Night Visitors

Cody watched Blake collect the pizza box and pop cans from the living room coffee table. "You don't have to do that, B," he called from the couch. "I was gonna clean it up later."

Blake smiled warmly. "It's okay, Code. I got it. I'm gonna toss this stuff, then head down the hall to your deluxe guest room. Gotta prep for Monday morning Bible study tomorrow."

Cody held his thumb on the TV remote's arrow key, trying to find a decent show. He thought Blake had retired to his temporary room, but he heard the exaggerated sound of someone clearing his throat.

Cody looked up. "You need to be tucked in or something, B? You're on your own if you do."

Blake nibbled his bottom lip. "Cody, my man," he began, "I get the feeling I'm kinda steppin' on your toes here. It's only my second day, uh, house-sitting or whatever, and I feel uncomfortable. And that's not the standard drill for you and me. I'm really not trying to cramp your style here, but I promised your dad that while he and Beth were on their honeymoon—"

Cody sighed. "Ah, B, I don't want you to feel bad. It's just that I'm almost fifteen. I don't need a babysitter. It's just ridiculous that Beth insisted on it, and I can't believe Dad didn't overrule her. Besides—"

Blake sat down in Luke Martin's recliner, which rested at a 90-degree angle from the couch. "Besides what, Cody?"

Cody sighed again. "It's just that when Dad and Beth get back from California, this house won't be the same again. Ever. It's gonna be louder. Busier. It's gonna be just plain trippy."

Cody saw Blake begin to nod slowly. "And you'd like to enjoy a few quiet evenings before everything changes—"

"Exactly."

Blake let his head tilt back toward the ceiling. "Oh, man, I don't know, Cody. I made a commitment to your dad—"

"—I won't say anything."

"C'mon, dude, you know we don't roll like that."

Cody sensed he was losing the argument. He leaned forward, rubbing his temples. "Well, how about this, then? You told my dad you'd look after me. That doesn't mean you have to be here *all* the time. He doesn't expect that anyway. He knows you have a demanding job—dealing with messed-up teens like me."

"And your point is?"

"Well, why don't you just pop in from time to time, just to check in and stuff? We can even have dinner every night, if you want. And I have your cell if there's an emergency."

"But, Code—"

"Blake, listen to me, please. I need some time to myself. *Need*, not just want. I'm not planning to have a drunken party over here or anything. You know me better than that."

Blake stood, frowning. Cody could almost see the tug-of-war going on in his head. "Tell you what," the youth pastor said finally. "Why don't we give your plan a try for tonight? See how things go."

Cody clapped his hands together. "Sounds like a plan to me."

"But you'll call me if anything comes up. If you start to feel—whatever. You can call me any time of the night."

"Will do, B."

Cody almost closed the door on Blake's backside as he ushered him out moments later.

Finally! Cody thought, as he plopped on the couch. *A little privacy. A little quiet.* He wondered how life would be when the new Mr. and Mrs. Martin returned in five days. Would Beth make breakfast every morning, the way his mom had? Would mornings be pleasant, yet quiet, the way he liked them? He hoped Beth wasn't one of those overly cheerful morning people, moving briskly, singing too loudly with the radio, saying stupid stuff like, "Smile, sunshine; it's a big, bright, brand-new day!"

"If Beth turns out to be a perky morning person," Cody mumbled, "I'm gonna have to join the army or the circus or something."

He padded to the refrigerator for a can of root beer. Upon his return, he collapsed in his father's chair, rested his feet on the coffee table, and chugged half the soda. He set the can down, to the left of one of the coasters Beth had purchased, and let out a long, satisfying belch. "Probably won't be able to do that much longer," he said ruefully.

After several minutes of channel surfing, Cody settled on a kung fu movie that seemed promising.

However, after an action-packed opening sequence, nearly twenty minutes chugged by without any "kung," and precious little "fu."

The last thing Cody remembered before he drifted to sleep was wishing he hadn't, in disgust, slid the remote to the opposite end of the coffee table—meaning he'd have to move from his comfortable position to retrieve it.

When his eyes popped open at 2:45 a.m., he began scrolling through his brain trying to think of a non-terrifying explanation for the sounds coming from his dad's bedroom upstairs.

The wind? No, the wind didn't shuffle coins or jewelry back and forth across the top of a chest of drawers—which constituted the sounds Cody was sure he heard. There was something purposeful about what was going on, as if someone were looking for something in particular. Like a burglar looking for the "good" jewelry. Cody shook his head briskly, trying to focus his thoughts. Did the Martins even own any good jewelry?

He sat rooted to the chair, willing the sounds to stop. *This can't be real*, he told himself. *This just can't be happening.*

Then something clunked to the floor. Too big to be an earring, too small to be a picture frame. A watch, maybe?

Cody scanned the area around him. *Man*, he scolded himself, *of all nights to have remembered to put the phone on the charger up in my room—instead of tossing it on the couch. Okay, then, that settles it. I'm out the front door, right now. Just as soon as I can get my legs to move.*

He felt sweat forming along his hairline. *C'mon*, he ordered himself. *Get moving. That burglar isn't going to stay up there forever. If it is a burglar. Could it be Gabe Weitz's brother? Whoever it is, you gotta move, dude!*

But for some reason he felt glued to the chair. He sucked in three deep breaths. *Okay, then, time to, as Blake would say, assess the situation. In fact, maybe it's Blake up there, just trying to scare me. Get back at me for booting him out—which I am now regretting with all my heart. I'll call up to him right now. Use my new, deeper puberty voice. Tell him I'm on to him.*

But when Cody opened his mouth, only a soft gasp escaped. He placed both palms on the arms of the chair and lifted himself up. Moving in slow motion, he eased his way to the front door and peered through the diamond-shaped window just below his eye level. There was no car in the driveway and nothing parked along the sidewalk either. He cupped his hand around the doorknob, ready to twist it and dash from the house.

Then he remembered Mom's wedding ring. Last he knew, it still rested in a jewelry box atop the chest of drawers. His dad kept saying he wanted to do something special with it, but he hadn't decided what.

Cody shook his head in disbelief. The ring was probably the only thing of value up there. The thief would be sure to take it. And Cody couldn't let that happen.

Moments later, Cody shuffled toward the staircase as if an invisible hand were pushing him. As he passed the smaller of two entryways from the living room into the kitchen, he noticed that the door leading into the kitchen from the garage stood ajar about a foot. *So that's how someone got in without noticing me, and vice versa*, he realized.

No way I should be doing this, he reminded himself as he reached the bottom step. *This is so not like me. But it's Mom's wedding ring we're talking about here. I don't think I could live with myself if I just let some creep walk outta here with it.* He stopped suddenly when the third step creaked under his left foot. He closed his mouth, allowing himself to breathe only through his nose. For a few seconds the rummaging sound stopped, then it resumed.

He reached the top of the stairs. The largest bedroom was about fifteen feet down a hallway to the left, just past Cody's room. He chastised himself for not picking up a weapon while he was downstairs. It was too late to go back now.

He moved along the wall on the same side as the bed-rooms, steadying himself with his left hand. *Be smart,* he warned himself. *Just make sure it's a burglar, not Blake or Pork Chop playing a joke, then you're outta here. At a neighbor's, calling the police.*

He startled for a moment when he heard an abrupt clicking sound, but then he stifled a sigh when he real-ized it was just the furnace coming on. He clenched his right fist as he eased forward again.

Cody knew he should pray, but, as often was the case when he was tempted to step into trouble, he didn't want to be accountable for the answer, which he fig-ured would reflect the advice in Matthew's gospel about earthly treasures versus heavenly treasures. He stopped when he reached his father's bedroom. There was still sound, but now it was coming from the bath-room off the bedroom.

I guess Mr. Burglar has moved on to new territory, maybe looking for Percodan or something. Slowly, Cody leaned his head into the bedroom doorway. There was definitely no one near the dresser now. He took two tentative steps into the room. He thought about dropping to his knees and crawling along the floor, as the king-size bed might shield him from view of whoever was in the bathroom. But, just as he was about to bend his knees, he sensed someone behind him.

Oh, heaven help me, he gulped. *There are two of 'em.*

Cody stood frozen. He didn't want to whip his head around suddenly, as that would surely bring an attack from behind. *Maybe if Burglar Number Two thinks I don't know he's there, he'll just stay put*, he reasoned. *So, Cody Martin, eyes front. Don't even think about looking behind you!*

Then Cody noticed the mirror. It was oval shaped, centered above the chest of drawers. *If I move just a little to my right*, he thought, *I might be able to see if anyone's behind me. Or if it's just my imagination.*

Cody pretended to merely shift his weight to the right, but as he did, he picked up his right foot and let it slide about eight inches. He felt his teeth clench as he strained to see what might be reflected behind him.

The figure was large, wearing some kind of long coat. Cody felt the top of his head tingle, as if being pricked by a thousand tiny needles. Without thinking, he wheeled around and drove his right fist right where he hoped the burglar's throat would be.

He punctuated the punch with an involuntary gorilla grunt, as he heard the figure hit the wall with a loud smack.

He was cocking his fist for a follow-up punch when he felt a sharp blow between his eyes.

Cody stood half-stunned and staring at the large shape in front of him. He wondered why he hadn't gone down when the blow struck him, especially when he realized that it was a board or club that hit him, not a human fist.

"Who are you?" he growled at his opponent—his voice choking its way through a mess of rage, frustration, and fear.

No reply came. Tentatively, Cody stepped forward. He thought of something Blake had said in youth group earlier in the week: "Sometimes, fear is God's microphone."

Okay, Lord, he confessed. *I'm hearing you, loud and clear. I'm sorry I didn't bounce outta here a long time ago. But since I'm here, please don't let this stubborn, silent thing in front of me be a ghost. Especially not the ghost of Gabe Weitz.*

He took a step backward, keeping his eyes fixed in front of him.

He laughed in spite of himself, as the scene came into focus. The sensation reminded of him when he used to watch *Wheel of Fortune* with his mom, and, suddenly, his mind would fill in the missing letters of a phrase or name.

It was his father's bathrobe. It hung from the back of the closet door on a temporary hanger that slid over the door's top. Cody usually found the robe wadded up on the bathroom floor or slung across an arm of the downstairs couch, but, obviously, the impending domestication was compelling Luke Martin to clean up his act. The closet door opened outward, so it was parallel to the wall when open all the way.

Cody rubbed the center of his forehead, chuckling again when he realized that his punch had caused the door to rebound off the wall, nearly putting a canyon down his skull. *At least it missed my nose*, he thought. *I already have five and a half zits; that's about all the imperfection my face can take at the moment. Anyway, big ups to you, Cody Martin. You're the first guy to beat up—himself!*

Cody felt his smile vanish when he heard more stirring from the bathroom. And his heart, which had only recently slowed enough so that he could feel each individual beat, accelerated again until his chest practically vibrated with a rapid-fire drum solo so fierce that he couldn't tell where one heartbeat ended and the next began. *I can't believe*, he scolded himself, *that I forgot about the other burglar—who I guess is the only burglar. But that's more than enough!*

He moved briskly to the doorway, risking one glance over his shoulder before he planned to descend all nine stairs with one bound and sprint all the way to—somewhere loud and bright and very, very public.

That's when he saw Miss Ella leap from the bathroom sink across the threshold of the bathroom.

"Oh, Miss Ella," he said, his voice quivering. "Y-you're behind all of this? You're gonna pay, big-time."

Miss Ella, who must have been patrolling the vanity in the bathroom, meowed and trotted toward Cody. Her purring intensified as she made figure eights through his legs, rubbing her lean body against his ankles.

"You scroungy feline," he said, with mock disgust. "You almost gave me a heart attack—not to mention almost making it necessary for me to change my underwear! That's the thanks I get for letting you come over and hang with me?"

Cody's dad was severely allergic to cats, as well as ragweed, pollen, dust mites, and so on. Whenever Cody's mom had completed medical forms for her husband, she replied "Pretty much everything" to questions about "known allergies."

So she and the then-sixth-grade Cody had conspired to covertly "adopt" Miss Ella, a midsize cat with a sleek gray coat, as a surrogate pet. Miss Ella's rightful owners, the Workmans down the street, didn't seem to pay much attention to her. They must have seen her lounging on the Martin porch or following Cody when he went to the mailbox, but they never came over and accused the Martins of trying to win their cat's affection and loyalty.

Miss Ella wasn't allowed in the Martin house. If Cody's dad had ever found cat hair on the couch, the game would have been up, and Miss Ella would be formally and finally banned from the premises. Occasionally, she managed to squirt between Cody's legs when he took out the trash, but either he or his mom would retrieve her before she was discovered.

Cody hadn't seen much of Miss Ella lately. Probably, he reasoned, because after his mom's death, the years-old tradition of sneaking the cat albacore tuna and whole milk on the back porch had all but vanished.

"Aw, Mom," Cody whispered softly as he tucked Miss Ella in his right arm and carried her like a football down the stairs, "even a stupid cat reminds me of you. It was fun, having a secret pet with you."

He gently set Miss Ella down on the front porch. "You head back to your real home, okay? I'll feed you some tuna this weekend. Sorry that I've been neglecting my duties."

Back in the house, Cody felt his still-tense muscles relax when Blake picked up the phone on the first ring. "Uh, B," he said tentatively, "I've been thinking, and I'm pretty sure my dad would be upset if you weren't over here, like physically, at night. I'm pretty sure he'd give me a lecture about following the letter of the law—as well as the spirit of the thing."

He heard Blake chuckling on the other end of the line. "What happened, Code? You watch a scary movie and get spooked or something?"

Cody erupted with a laugh that he hoped didn't sound as fake as it felt. "Yeah, right, Blake. You think a stupid TV show can scare me? Ha!"

Cody hung up the phone. "A bathrobe, now *that's* another story," he said.

Chapter 7

Captain Cody?

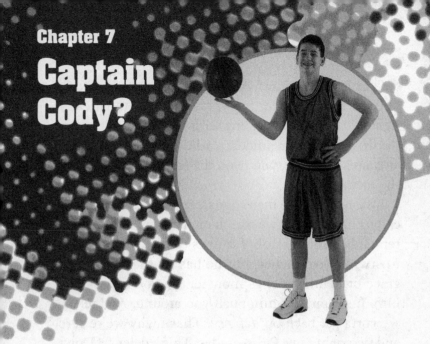

The locker room buzzed with nervous energy. Outside, Cody could hear the cheers rising occasionally as Robyn and the frosh girls battled their longtime rivals from Holy Family. *There's nothing like the home opener*, Cody thought, as he watched Bart Evans make his fourth or fifth trip to the urinals, passing Slaven, Sam Hooper, and Gannon on the way.

Mark Goddard, short on height and talent but big on desire, sat on a bench near the entrance bouncing a ball firmly between his legs. The slap-slap of leather on cement seemed to set the backbeat for all the activity.

Coach Clayton moved to the center of the room. "Listen up," he said, his voice uncharacteristically tight. "To start, we're going with Bart and Brett at forwards, Slaven in the middle, and Goddard and Gannon at guards. Gannon, you're on the point, so take care of the rock.

"We're gonna go man to man on this team. Athletically, I like the way we match up with 'em. Slaven, you remember Young, Holy Family's center? He's shot up to six feet five inches, but he has all the agility and grace of Frankenstein's monster. So you can handle him. Just don't let him push you around. And fellas, we gotta get back on *defense*. That's why we're zero and two right now. Please, fellas. Think defense! Don't make me beg."

The team hit the court for warm-ups. Cody heard a sprinkling of applause. He scanned the stands and felt his spirits deflate at the sparse crowd. After drawing full houses in the cramped middle-school gym the previous season, this was a letdown.

"I bet the chess team packs in a better crowd than this," he grumbled.

"Let's get some layups in," Brett Evans called out.

"Nah," his brother countered. "Let's just shoot around for a while. Get loosened up."

Cody saw Brett's eyes narrow as he stared down Bart. "Coach said layups first."

"Well, I didn't hear him."

"That's because you weren't listening, as usual! Some cocaptain you are!"

"Hey," Cody offered, "let's compromise and do tip drills."

Gannon brushed past Cody, grabbing the ball from his hands. "Don't let me interrupt your little sewing circle," he said, his voice dripping sarcasm. "But I'm gonna shoot some buckets."

Cody shrugged and jogged to the Eagle bench and plucked another ball from the stainless-steel rack on wheels. The rest of the team followed suit.

Cody had just missed his fifth straight shot from the left wing when the buzzer sounded, meaning it was game time. *Woulda been nice to make at least one shot*, he complained to himself. *Just to prove I can still shoot. Of course, I woulda sunk at least two or three if Gannon hadn't shot at the same time and messed up my shots. What does it matter anyway? I'll probably spend half the game on the bench. I can't believe Coach didn't make me a starter right away. Has he forgotten I made all-tournament team last year?*

Cody slumped at the end of the bench and watched Holy Family go on a 13–0 run to start the game. Keenan Jones took Bart to school on the first three Saint possessions, and, despite Coach Clayton's pregame admonitions, Young dominated Slaven on the low post. If it had been Pork Chop at center, the story would have been different. But Pork Chop was playing JV ball. It had taken only three practices for the JV coach to wrest him from Coach Clayton's clutches. He had notched eighteen points and fifteen boards (and four personal fouls and a warning for a technical foul) in his first junior varsity game. By midseason, Cody estimated, Chop would join Alston on the varsity.

As the Eagle frosh jogged off the court at the end of the first quarter, Cody stared at Coach Clayton, whose narrow face was etched in a frown. "Just dandy, kiddies," the coach said. "We're down 16–2— to a team we whupped by 14 last year. Now, math never was my strong suit, but I do believe that makes us about 28 points worse. Did you guys forget everything I taught you last season? This is the most disgusting thing I've seen since my ex-mother-in-law donned a two-piece bathing suit at a family reunion. All y'all so-called starters can take a seat. I'm clearing my bench; second five in, now!"

As Cody headed to the scorer's table to check into the game, Coach Clayton hooked him by the elbow. "Dawg," he whispered loudly, "how 'bout stopping with the sulking, getting your head in the game, and starting with some leadership?"

The words stung Cody. For a moment, he thought about protesting his coach's sarcasm. Then he saw his four teammates wandering onto the court looking like immigrants stepping on US soil for the first time.

"Listen up," Cody said, approaching them. "Jones is all mine. Hooper, you take Young. And don't be afraid to front him. Wright, you help Hoop if he gets beaten down low. Lang, overplay Mack to his right. He's got no left hand. Berringer, it looks like they're putting in a new guy at two-guard—you got him. C'mon, let's get back in this!"

Almost as one, Cody's four teammates stared at him and shrugged. *They're probably wondering who died and made me boss*, he reasoned. *But that's okay. I'm not having us go out and get spanked like the starters— in our house! This is downright embarrassing!*

Holy Family got the ball to start the quarter. Mack drove right, then looked to lob to Young on the low block. Hooper fought his way in front of the much larger center and, after tipping the pass once, gained control of the ball.

"Outlet, Hoop!" Cody barked at the backup center, holding his hands out. Hooper fired a chest pass to Cody, who immediately looked downcourt and spotted a streaking Berringer. Cody cocked his right arm and hurled a football-style pass—right over Berringer's head.

"Well, John Elway I am not," Cody scolded himself, punctuating his remark with a slap across his thigh.

As he backpedaled into defensive position, he heard Coach Clayton yelling, "That's the right idea, fellas! Keep it up! Keep it up!"

On the Saints' next possession, Mack was successful in lobbing the ball over Hooper's up-stretched hands.

"Help!" hollered Cody.

Quickly, Wright left his opponent and slid into position behind Young. When the big center turned toward the basket, he was surprised to find reinforcements in his way. Moments later, he was whistled for too much time in the lane.

Cody pulled alongside Lang as they ran downcourt to set up on offense. "Mack's giving you lots of room," he said. "He knows you're too quick for him."

Bradley Lang nodded. He called for the ball as soon as Berringer brought it across half-court. As Lang dribbled toward Mack on the left wing, the Saint guard gave ground, his hands low. Lang stopped quickly and elevated for a sixteen-footer that orbited the rim once before dropping in.

After consecutive blocks by Hooper and Cody led to Berringer fast-break layups, Holy Family's coach ejected from his chair and signaled a time-out.

"We got 'em running scared," Lang said, smiling at Cody as they trotted to the sideline.

"Maybe," Cody said grimly, "but we're still getting waxed, 16–8."

"You so-called starters taking note of this?" Coach Clayton said, staring down his first five with accusing eyes. The Evans brothers nodded sullenly. Slaven studied his shoes as if they were the most interesting items in the entire gym. Gannon and Goddard stared straight ahead, eyes smoldering.

"Well," the coach continued after a few uncomfortable seconds dragged by, "keep watching and learning. Second five, stay on the court."

Holy Family got its first points of the quarter when Jones converted both ends of a one-and-one, but Grant slammed the door after that. The period ended with the Saints clinging to an 18–17 lead.

Cody jogged to the locker room expecting halftime praise for the second unit—and a hailstorm of criticism for the starters. Coach Clayton, however, said nothing until just before the team trotted out of the locker room. "We'll go with our starters again to start the third," he said quietly.

As Slaven and Young squared off for the second-half jump ball, Coach Clayton patted the chair next to him. "Martin," he said, his voice ragged and weary, "right here, dawg."

Cody whistled sadly through his teeth as he watched Holy Family stretch its lead to ten points. Jones set a beautiful back pick for Mack, and the latter returned the favor moments later. Young earned a three-point play when he head faked Slaven into the air, then banked in a shot from close range.

When Mack hit an uncontested three-pointer from the top of the key, Cody wondered if his coach might bolt onto the court and drag his lackluster starting five to the sidelines. Instead, he just sighed and turned to Cody. "You see what's happening out there, don't you, dawg?"

"Yeah. A massacre."

The coach snorted. "That's a pretty apt description. But why?"

Cody looked away from Coach Clayton for a moment, turning his eyes to center court where the Evans twins seemed to be arguing over who would assume the unenviable task of guarding Keenan Jones. "Well, I'm not sure, Coach, but it looks like nobody wants to take charge out there."

"You get a gold star, Cody Martin," Coach Clayton said, his voice resonating with disgust. "For the love of Larry Bird, nobody wants to be a leader. What we've got out there are five guys playing as individuals, not as a team. Nobody wants to be accountable for bringing 'em together—the way you were with the second five."

Cody smacked his hands together in frustration as Gannon launched a twenty-footer, missing Brett Evans wide open under the basket. "Somebody's gotta tell him to have a look down low," he shouted.

Coach Clayton smiled. "Yeah, *somebody* sure does. You get yourself in there and do it."

"But, Coach," Cody stammered, "Bart and Brett are captains; they're not gonna listen to me. Besides—"

"Besides what, dawg? Captain ain't some honorary title. It's all about what you *do*. To me, captain is a verb. And Evans & Evans, Incorporated, aren't doin' jack—except carping at each other."

"But Coach, I've never been a team captain. I'm really not comfortable hollering at guys and stuff—"

"Comfortable? You think I care if you're comfortable? Dawg, I'm your coach, not your flight attendant. And right now, your coach—your team—needs a leader. So get your skinny carcass out there and lead!"

Cody checked into the game on the next dead ball. As the Eagles settled into defensive position, Cody barked, "Call out the picks! And don't be afraid to holler help if you get beaten on D. C'mon, fellas, we gotta talk on defense!"

Holy Family's rail-thin backup point guard attacked the right wing trying to set up a pick-and-roll with Jones. "Switch!" Cody called as he watched Jones plant himself behind Gannon. Gannon nodded, then rolled right along with Jones as he moved toward the basket.

Cody, meanwhile, jumped out on the point guard, smothering him, frustrating him, until the referee blew his whistle. "Five-second violation," he intoned.

As Gannon walked the ball upcourt on Grant's ensuing possession, Cody saw the Saint guard creeping up behind him ready to steal the ball.

"Wolf right! Wolf right!" Cody barked, using the code term Coach Clayton had taught his team last year.

Gannon smiled and deftly crossed his dribble from his right hand to his left. The Holy Family defender sped by, swatting at nothing but air.

Grant finished quarter number three up by two points. The Eagles extended the lead to eight midway into the fourth—with Cody and the second team seeing most of the action.

Coach Clayton called a time-out with 3:49 left in the game, putting his original starters back in. *That's a good move*, Cody thought, nodding approvingly. *I bet by now they're learned their lesson. And maybe I showed Bart and Brett at least a little about how to be a captain.*

As the clock ticked away to less than a minute, Cody caught himself frowning at his coach. *Why doesn't he call time-out?* he wondered. *Holy Family is pummeling us again. Why doesn't he put the second five back*

in? We're gonna lose this game—our home opener! This stinks!

Cody looked down the bench. Judging from their expressions, his teammates shared his bewilderment. Cody shrugged, then slumped in his chair, arms folded across his chest.

The locker room was noiseless—like quiet prayer time during church. Holy Family had won by six, making the victory look much easier than the score indicated.

Cody waited until all of his teammates had left the locker room before sliding next to Coach Clayton, who was sitting on a bench near the showers, pressing his head between his hands, like a vise.

"Coach," he said softly, "can I talk with you?"

"Not if you're gonna complain about playing time or something like that," the coach said wearily. "If anyone's gonna gripe and moan about the game, it oughta be me."

Cody nibbled on his bottom lip. "Well, it's not really my PT that has me confused, but—"

Coach Clayton arched his eyebrows. "But?"

Cody let a long, slow sigh escape his lungs. "Well, I'm not trying to be disrespectful or anything, but I kinda feel like we let the game get away tonight."

"Not 'we,' Martin. I. I let the game get away. Isn't that what you mean?"

Cody felt his head nodding. He willed it to stop, but he didn't seem to be in control of his nodding muscles.

Coach Clayton smiled. "An honest man. I like that. And you're not just honest, you're right."

Cody stopped—in midnod. "But, Coach, I don't understand. We threw a game?"

"Not 'threw.' Sacrificed. And don't look at me with that constipated face, dawg. You play baseball. You know what a sacrifice is. A guy is willing to get an out, in order to advance a runner. You give up a little thing to get something bigger."

Cody tried to erase the constipated expression from his face before speaking. "But we lost, Coach. What could be bigger than that?"

"The rest of the season, my man. Think about it: If we had won, do you think half the knuckleheads on this team would have remembered how pathetically we played for most of the game? But dropping our home opener—and our third game in a row? Believe me, this sting will stay with everyone for quite a while. And, I hope—I dearly hope—the sting will help us remember *why* we lost. And you know that 'why.' Lack of leadership, plain and simple. Lack of Cody Martin leadership."

"But Coach," Cody began to protest, "Brett and Bart have played basketball longer than I have. They've been to camps, and—"

Coach Clayton clapped his hands together. The smacking sound echoed in Cody's ears. "I've had a gut full of the But Coach whinin' from you, Mr. Martin. You're not sure you can lead this team—this whole team. I can see that in your eyes. You were good enough to lead my defense last year—and my second string this year. But you're not sure about the whole enchilada.

"So you listen up. I've seen you carrying that big ol' industrial-strength Bible around school lately. That baby's gotta contain the Old Testament as well as the New. And it's been a while since I studied the Good Book, but I seem to recall this dude named Moses who said 'But Coach God—waa-waaa-waa-waaa!' when he was asked to be a leader. He whined, 'Make my brother Bart the boss. He's better than I am. He talks better—and he has a better jump shot!' Sound familiar?"

Cody smiled and nodded. "Yeah, it sounds familiar. Except his brother was Aaron, not Bart."

"I knew that," Coach Clayton said, standing. "I was testing you. So, we got East in a couple of days, at their place. You gonna be ready, Captain Martin?"

Cody smiled at his coach. "I'll be ready."

Coach Clayton patted him on the head. "Aw, for the love of Moses—and Moses Malone—I hope so. 'Cuz this losing stuff—it stinks like three-day-old roadkill!"

Cody stood alone in Grant High's small auxiliary gym holding his traveling bag. He felt the throbbing in his head subsiding. The locker room had been too noisy. *I'm glad to be outta there,* he thought. The Evans twins were feuding about something, Slaven was pacing up and down singing loudly and off-key to whatever music he had going on his MP3. Gannon, meanwhile, was stalking about trying to snap his teammates with a wet towel someone must have left after a PE class. Cody was in no mood to be snapped. He feared that if Gannon came after him, he'd end up wrapping the towel around Gannon's neck, and the frosh Eagles stood no chance of ending their three-game losing streak with a strangled point guard.

Cody took a few deep breaths. *Okay, time to get back in there. Maybe things have settled down by now. Time to help Coach round up everybody and get 'em on the bus to East.*

From the opening tip of the East game, Cody tried to will his team to victory. He took on the toughest defensive assignment, the fiery, ultra-athletic Bobby Cabrera, called out picks on defense, and constantly sprinted into the backcourt to help Gannon when he was double-teamed.

Most of the team seemed to be accepting his leadership, but he felt icy glares from the Evans twins every time he directed a comment or barked a command toward one of them. They had stared daggers at Coach Clayton when, in the visitors' locker room before the game, he announced Cody Martin as the new team captain—and that initial resentment showed little sign of fading.

When Brett and Bart weren't challenging Cody, they were sniping at each other—for failing to help on defense, for not giving up the rock on fast breaks, and even over who would sit closest to Coach Clayton on the bench.

The frosh Eagles battled East right down to the last possession, but when Cody fouled out with 1:34 left in the game, Bobby Cabrera took over. He was too quick for Goddard, and East eked out a three-point win.

In the uneasy silence of the visitors' locker room, the now 0–4 Eagles peeled off uniforms, showered, and dressed quickly. Some stuffed their sweaty uniforms in their travel bags. Cody, as his mom had always insisted, placed his uniform on a hanger to let it air out a bit on the bus ride home.

Cody followed Goddard out of the locker room. The slightly portly guard's round face was still flushed, and he moved with a slight limp, as a result of taking a knee to the meatiest part of his right thigh while trying to get around a pick and stay with Cabrera on defense.

Cody studied his teammate and felt a flicker of admiration. *Goddard played harder than anybody tonight,* he thought. *In fact, he's the only one who played hard for the whole game. Maybe Coach should make him captain. Maybe Brett and Bart would respect him, for his work ethic, if nothing else. They're sure never gonna respect me. Neither will Gannon. Of course, he's too much of a knucklehead to respect anybody. I think I'll talk to Coach on Monday, tell him I resign as captain.*

Cody rehearsed his resignation speech all weekend. He arrived at school at 6:15 so he'd be sure to have time to tell Coach Clayton the news before anyone else arrived.

He found the coach in the gym shooting free throws. "Aw, for the love of Chris Dudley," Coach Clayton moaned, as his shot bounced off the back iron, "that was one ugly shot."

Cody cleared his throat. The coach turned his head. "Oh, hey, dawg. I hope you didn't see that brick I just threw up. To tell you the truth, I've been throwing up more bricks than a mason's convention. Don't tell anybody, though, or I'll have you runnin' suicides till your feet fall off!"

Cody nodded. "Uh, Coach, you got a minute?"

Coach Clayton frowned. "To tell you the truth, Mr. Martin, I'm fresh outta minutes. I got something important to tend to before practice. So why don't you take this ball here and see if you can bust through the lid someone musta put over the basket."

"But Coach—"

"But nothin', numb-noggin. You may be captain of the team, but I'm the general. So you go ahead and do what I just told you." With that, he flipped the ball to Cody and jogged toward the locker room.

"We'll have a special guest joining us this morning," Coach Clayton told his team after they had completed warm-ups and stretching. He raised his voice. "Uh, Mr. Special Guest, you can quit lurking by the exit and join us now."

Terry Alston sulked into the gym, head bowed. Gannon looked to Cody and shrugged. Cody returned the gesture with his best "don't look at me" facial expression.

Coach Clayton seemed to be enjoying his team's reactions. He waited several moments before intoning, "It seems our varsity coach was not pleased with Mr. Alston's five-turnover, four-foul, one-point, zero-assist performance last week. I believe I heard the admonition: 'Alston, if you're gonna play like a stinkin' freshman, you can start practicing with the freshmen!'"

Alston was muttering something to himself, but Cody couldn't decipher it.

"Now, I'm not sure I appreciate my fellow coach impugning my team's ability," Coach Clayton continued, "but, given the way we've played, I'm not sure I can find fault in his assessment. In any case, Mr. Alston was a teammate to most of you last year, so I trust you'll make him welcome—but not too welcome. He's here to get a workout."

Alston stretched out while the frosh went through layup drills. He finally joined them as they began tip drills.

Cody had to stifle a grin as he watched Alston, puffy-eyed and sporting a serious case of bed head, go through the motions like an extra in a zombie movie. He considered tossing a few encouraging words to his former teammate, but Alston didn't look like he wanted to be encouraged. He looked like he wanted to be back in bed.

Cody didn't think much about Alston until late in the practice when Coach Clayton said he wanted to spend twenty minutes scrimmaging. He put Alston with Bart, Brett, Gannon, and Hooper—meaning Cody would have to captain a pack of second-teamers. *Way to stack the odds against us, Coach*, he thought, hoping Mr. Clayton could read his mind.

"By the way," Coach Clayton said, before setting the game clock, "losing team runs suicides after practice. Winners get to shower early."

Cody wasn't sure if it was the threat of suicides or just Alston's wanting to show the other freshmen how much better he was, but the scrimmage brought Zombie Alston fully to life. Paired against Goddard, he screamed for the ball every time, bellowing "Mismatch! I got a mismatch! Get me the rock!"

On his fivesome's first three possessions, Alston head faked Goddard into the air, then drove past him for easy layups.

Then, after Lang missed a baseline jumper, Alston snagged the rebound and bolted downcourt, Goddard scrambling to stay with him. Alston angled toward the basket, rose gracefully into the air, pushing a leaping Goddard off with his left hand, and floated in a teardrop shot with his right hand. "Eat that, doughboy!" he spat at Goddard as the ball whispered through the net.

As Goddard sprinted back to play offense, Cody thought he could see tears forming in his eyes.

After Cody closed the gap to 8–2 with a driving left-handed layup over Bart, Alston answered with an assist to Brett—via a pass between Goddard's legs. Then, as he moved to the rim for a possible offensive rebound, Alston drove an elbow into Goddard's stomach.

Cody felt his face grow hot. He pulled next to Alston as both of them ran down the court. "You didn't have to do that," he said.

Alston shrugged. "Basketball's a contact sport. If Goddard can't take it, there's always room in the band."

Marcus Berringer fired up a wild shot, and Alston pushed Goddard all the way past the baseline before hauling in the rebound.

Cody looked to Coach Clayton as he hunkered down to play defense. The coach slitted his eyes at his captain. *I know what you're wondering, Coach,* he thought. *How many times am I gonna let my teammate get abused? Well, I'm wondering the same thing myself.*

Meanwhile, Alston had isolated Goddard on the right wing. He jab-stepped left—and Goddard eagerly went for the fake, moving himself out of defensive position. Alston had a clear path to the basket. He didn't have to bounce the ball off of Goddard's forehead just to humiliate him further, but that's what he did.

Cody nearly spat on the court in disgust. He left Bart on the left wing and charged at Alston.

If Alston had shot a simple right-handed layup, Cody would have been too late to defend it. But Alston had decided to get cute, crossing under the basket for a reverse layup from the left side. That gave Cody the time he needed. He heard himself grunt with effort as he launched his body into the air. He extended his right arm and swatted the ball off the lower corner of the backboard.

But the ball wasn't all that Cody hit. He felt his right hip bone strike Alston in his exposed flank. The startled point guard stumbled backward, crashing into the padding on the wall behind the basket.

Cody raised his hand, acknowledging the foul. A hard but clean foul. A message foul.

Alston stood for a moment with his back plastered to the protective mat, blinking. Then he charged forward. His eyes locked on Cody. "That was a cheap shot, Martin! I mean, you wanna go, then let's go. But don't cheap-shot me!"

Cody stood his ground. "That wasn't a cheap shot," he said, struggling to keep his voice from quaking. "That was a warning. Your second warning: Don't punk out my teammate."

Alston raised his fists. "Enough with the talk, Martin!"

Cody swallowed hard and, tentatively, raised his fists too.

Cody winced as the shrill blast of Coach Clayton's whistle invaded his ears.

"Whoa there, Mr. Alston," coach said, inserting himself between the two opponents, "you better lower those things unless you're really ready to use 'em."

Alston stared at the coach. "Are you *kiddin'* me?"

Coach Clayton smiled cryptically. "I never kid about player-on-player violence. I'm just recommending that you think about what you're doin.' You come into our house and keep goin' after a guy you got on the ropes. You think my captain is gonna stand for that?"

"Martin? A captain?" Alston snorted.

Coach Clayton nodded. "Yeah. Cody Martin—a captain. My captain. Mark Goddard's captain. And if you wanna scrap with my captain, I hope you brought a lunch, 'cuz you're gonna be here all day. Ain't that right, dawg?" Cody looked at Goddard, then at Alston, and, finally, at his coach. "All day and all night, Coach," he said.

Alston rolled his eyes. "Whatever. Let's just play ball."

Cody nodded. "That's a good suggestion. But, Coach, I have a request: I'm guarding Alston now."

Coach Clayton couldn't contain his smile. "That didn't sound like a request, dawg. That sounded like an order."

Alston committed an intentional charging foul on Cody the first time he got a chance, lowering his shoulder for extra impact. Cody popped to his feet as quickly as he could, willing his facial muscles to register no emotion, no pain.

On Cody's next defensive sequence, Alston beat him along the baseline and bolted toward the basket. Cody quickly recovered and bore down behind the quick guard. Alston elevated for a soft floater, and Cody leaped up and forward to block the shot. As he sailed past his opponent, he thought he saw Alston flinch. He left the shot short. Goddard dashed in for the rebound, flashing Cody a quick smile.

"Terry Alston—intimidated," he whispered. "I never thought I'd see the day."

Alston's squad won the scrimmage, 20–14, but Cody didn't feel like a loser when it was over—especially because of the way his team scored its final two points. With only twelve seconds left in the scrimmage, Gannon tossed a lazy pass toward Alston. Cody deflected the ball away, then chased it across half-court for an easy breakaway layup. No one on Alston's team bothered to give chase.

One player did follow Cody: Mark Goddard. As was his custom, he refused to give up on a play. Cody risked a quick glance behind him as he angled in for a layup. When he saw Goddard trailing him, he stopped, waited, and dished the ball off to his teammate. Goddard missed his first layup, but he followed his shot and scored the scrimmage's final points as time expired.

Cody chest-bumped him as the ball trickled through the net. "Nice shot, dude," he said.

"Thanks," Goddard said, eyes grateful. "For everything. Man, I thought Brett and Bart's jaws were gonna hit the floor when you faced off with Alston!"

Coach Clayton waited until Alston's team trotted to the locker room before addressing Cody's team. "Good comeback, fellas. But a deal's a deal. It's suicide time. How many do you think we need, Captain Martin?"

Cody stroked his chin. "I'm thinking at least one, Coach."

Coach Clayton bobbed his head. "That sounds reasonable. Just don't run it too hard, men. We got one more game before Christmas break, and I don't want anyone spraining an ankle."

Chapter 8

Showdowns

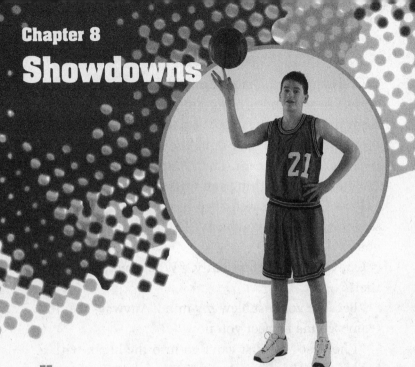

Un-beeeee-lievable," Pork Chop said for the fourth or fifth time, as he wedged his foot into a size eleven Nike.

Cody tried to suppress a smile. "It was no big deal, Chop. I was just standing up for a teammate, you know."

"Yeah, but standing up to Terry Alston? Bro, that's fierce! I'm surprised he didn't beat you down to the size of that Mini Me dude."

"Well, after practice, he did get in my face—told me I was lucky to still own all my teeth."

Pork Chop's mouth dropped open. "And?"

Cody shrugged. "I told him, 'I know. But regardless of the consequences, a captain has to be down for his teammates. It's what Blake calls servant leadership.' I told him I would have done the same thing for him, if he were on my team. Then Alston looks at me like I'm crazy or something and walks away."

Pork Chop appeared deep in thought. "Code," he said finally, "I bet you blew Alston's mind with what you said."

Cody frowned skeptically. "What makes you say that?"

"Because you just blew *my* mind. Anyway, I bet the team's gonna respect you now."

"I hope so. We just can't go into the break with a big bagel in the win column."

Pork Chop stood. "Well, have a good practice— over in the little baby gym."

Cody chuckled. "Hey, I'm just glad that volleyball season is over so we can have the auxiliary gym after school now. Anything's better than practicing at 6:30 in the morning!"

After practice, Cody trotted toward the showers. He had promised his dad and Beth he would be in the parking lot no later than six o'clock. He almost collided with Robyn, which, given that he was dripping sweat, wouldn't have been a good thing.

"Hey, Cody," she said. "Tough practice?"

He tried to will himself to stop sweating. "Yeah. Friday's the last game before Christmas break. Last chance to get a W this year. We're all feeling the pressure."

"Yeah," she said quietly. "I kinda get the feeling you're feeling the pressure over a lot of things." Then she moved her right hand from behind her back and thrust it toward Cody's face.

"Here," she said, holding a folded-up piece of note-book paper on her palm. "This is for you."

Cody frowned. "For me? Why?"

She smiled at him. "Paul, our new youth pastor, gave us an assignment last week. He read Hebrews 3:13, you know, the verse that says 'Encourage one another daily'? Then he asked us to think of someone who needed to be encouraged. And, of course, I thought of you."

Of course? Cody thought. *Of course she thought of me? Cool! Then again, maybe that only means I'm the most pathetic person she knows.*

He heard Robyn clear her throat. "So, do you want it or not?"

"Oh, s-sorry," he stammered. "Yeah, sure. Thanks."

He plucked the paper from her hand. "So, this is, like, something you wrote?"

She rolled her eyes. "No, it's something I baked. Can't you smell it?"

He felt the urge to squirm out of his own skin and disappear down the nearest drain. *Good, smart question, Cody,* he scolded himself. *Way to think on your feet.*

"Anyway," she was saying, "it's kinda free-form poetry or whatever. It's not exactly Mother Goose. If you think it stinks or whatever, you can just throw it away and forget this whole thing ever happened."

"No—I'm sure I'll like it, Hart. Thanks—again." He turned and headed for the locker room. He pulled back his shoulders and straightened his spine as he walked. He wanted to make himself taller, just in case she was watching.

Cody held the folded-up paper against his leg as he entered the locker room. *Can't let anyone see this,* he thought. *Especially now that all the JV and varsity guys are here too. That's all I need is for one of them to notice. Chop will confiscate it, stand on a bench, and read it to the whole team.*

Feeling a new sweat coming over him—a nervous sweat, not an athletic one—he fumbled with his lock, almost chastising himself out loud when his haste caused him to miss the third number in his combination.

He exhaled in relief when he felt the lock give way on his second attempt. He poked his hand in the locker and tucked the note into the back pocket of his jeans.

Man, I'd give anything to know what it says, he thought as he unlaced his shoes. He tried to think of the last time a girl had passed him a note. To the best of his recollection, it was fourth grade, when Jill Keller had presented him with a homemade, one-question multiple-choice quiz:

Do you like me?

Yes____   No _____   Maybe _____

It was the hardest quiz Cody had taken up to that point in life. He had made up a fourth choice—"As a Friend"—then marked it and returned it to Jill via one of her friends. Jill didn't speak to him for two weeks.

But eventually she had turned her fourth-grade affection to Pork Chop. He checked "Yes" on *his* note, and Cody was forgotten, if not forgiven.

Pork Chop and Jill lasted about a mo grew tired of sharing him with half th grade.

Cody caught himself smiling at the recolle Jill and Robyn were best friends now. He wondered i

Jill had ever told Robyn about her brief infatuation with him. If she even remembered it.

"You forget how to get out of your gear?"

Pork Chop's voice invaded Cody's thoughts, and he hoped his friend didn't notice that he had startled at the sound of it.

"Oh, hey, Chop. Good practice?"

Pork Chop nodded. "Dawg, we are so ready for Claxton Hills. We're gonna put a whuppin' on 'em—get revenge for football."

Cody whistled through his teeth. "I hope so. But those guys are good."

"So are we."

Pork Chop paused for a few moments, then said, "So, Code, what's on your mind? You looked like you were contemplating the meaning of the universe just now."

Cody tried to laugh nonchalantly. "Oh, it's nothing, Chop. I'm just kinda tired, I guess."

"Yeah, I'm *sure* that's what's up." Chop was smiling like he knew a secret.

Man, Cody marveled to himself. *This guy reads me l̶i̶k̶e̶ ̶I̶ ̶u̶s̶e̶d̶ to read defenses.*

̶H̶e̶ ̶t̶r̶i̶e̶d̶ ̶t̶o̶ keep from tumbling into his locker ̶a̶s̶ ̶C̶h̶o̶p̶ clapped him across the back. "Anyway, ̶i̶f̶ you wanna kick it, you know where to find me."

Cody took the shortest shower of his life. He studied his watch, which read 5:56. Only four minutes to find a private place, read Robyn's poem, then sprint to the parking lot so that he wouldn't be late and suffer his dad's glaring at him all the way home—and all through dinner.

He bolted from the locker room and into the large restroom in the gym lobby. He locked himself in a stall and retrieved the paper from his pocket. *Well*, he thought as he unfolded Robyn's handiwork, *this isn't the most artistic setting in which to read poetry*, but *at least it's* way *private.*

The piece was titled "For a Friend." He hoped it wouldn't make him cry. It had been at least three days since he cried—when the Martins had dinner guests and his dad happily announced Beth as "my wonderful wife." The same way he used to introduce the first Mrs. Martin.

Cody took a deep breath and began reading Robyn's carefully rendered lettering.

You've seen things that most can't see,
  done things most can't dream.

You have dreams you fear won't last,
  because you fear you won't succeed.

But you already have.

You keep looking back, into the past,
    at what you've lost—reliving old pain.
Turn around, look ahead of you,
    and you'll see how much you've gained.

I know that you still have some wounds
    that only hope can heal.
I know it's hard to open up
    and tell me how you feel.

I'll remember to be patient,
    if you'll hold on to hope,
    and remember, too, you're in my prayers
    no matter where you go.

"Wow, Hart," he whispered. "No one's ever written a poem for me. Guess I'll have to keep runnin' with you in the mornings—no matter how cold it gets."

"Did practice go okay, dude?" Beth asked, studying him in the rearview mirror.

"Yeah, it was pretty good."

"Really?" Beth's voice was tinged with suspicion. "Because you look like you just scarfed some bad egg salad or something."

Cody forced a smile. "Is there such a thing as *good* egg salad?" he asked.

Beth giggled, perhaps a bit too hard. "Point taken," she said. "But, Cody, I can tell you're carrying a lot of weight inside. If you need someone to help with the heavy lifting, I am here for you. I'm always gonna be here, you know?"

Yeah, Cody thought. *And that's the problem. Well, not THE problem, but it's definitely in the top ten.*

The rumor began spreading, like smoke, through the freshman team at Thursday's practice. Central's frosh team, which was 5–0 on the young season, was serious about going into the holiday break with its perfect record intact. And as insurance, Rick Macy would be making the trip to Grant.

"Well, there goes our chance of getting a W this year," Gannon grumbled as he stood behind Cody in a layup line. "Macy scored fourteen for the *varsity* a couple weekends ago. I can't believe they're gonna let him go against us."

"Well," Cody said, "it's only a rumor."

"Yeah," Gannon countered, "like Pork Chop's moving away is just a rumor. But that's true, isn't it?"

Cody felt pressure on his chest, as if someone were bear-hugging him. "Chop doesn't like to talk about it. But, yeah, after the school year, he could be gone."

"There you go," Gannon said as he took off toward the basket. "Sometimes rumors are true."

Gannon proved prophetic. As he led his team onto the court to warm up, Cody looked to the opposite end of the gym and saw Macy launching long-range jumpers from the baseline. His baggy shorts hung so low on his hips that Cody wondered what held them up.

Coach Clayton wasn't fond of loose-fitting uniforms. He didn't make his team wear old-school John Stockton short shorts, but he insisted, "None of my players are gonna be running around in drawers ten times too big. This is basketball, not some hip-hop fashion show. You keep them drawers pulled up, jerseys tucked in."

Cody almost shuddered as he and Macy met at half-court for pregame instructions from the lead referee. *It's like shaking hands with a Komodo dragon*, Cody thought.

But while his handshake was creepy, Macy's face bore a smile. "I thought you'd be playing JV at least, Martin," he said.

Cody shrugged. "Not ready yet, I guess."

"You gonna be guarding me?"

"Trying to, anyway."

Macy nodded approvingly. "And so it begins again—"

Cody chuckled to himself as he jogged toward Coach Clayton and the team. "'And so it begins again?' Macy's been playing too many medieval video games," he said.

Grant started fast. Cody sensed that Miller, Central's six-three post man, would outjump Slaven, so he leaped in front of Macy and stole the opening tip. His pass to Gannon was a bit long, but the freckle-faced guard chased it down and scored on an uncontested layup.

Neither team led by more than four points in the first half. Cody attached himself to Macy like a leech as he darted all over the court, trying to free himself for a clean look at the basket. Macy finished the half with six points, on three of nine shooting, staking Central to a 24–22 lead.

Central stretched the margin to four as the third quarter ended, with Miller doing most of the damage close to the basket.

Slaven picked up his fourth foul early in the final period, then fouled out at the 5:51 mark. Coach

Clayton called time-out and put Brett Evans on
Miller. "Y'all are gonna have to box out," he told his
team, "or Miller's gonna gobble up every stinkin'
rebound."

On Grant's next possession, Gannon narrowed
Central's lead to 38–36 with a three-pointer from the
top of the key.

The teams traded baskets and free throws for the
next two minutes, but in the process, Brett Evans was
tagged with his fourth foul.

With just over three-and-a-half minutes in the game
and the Eagles trailing 43–41, Coach Clayton called
another time-out.

"Listen, fellas," Cody panted, injecting his voice
with as much authority as he could muster. "If Macy
gets into the lane, don't be afraid to foul him."

Brett stared at Cody in disbelief. Cody knew what his
teammate was thinking—Macy was almost automatic
from the free throw line.

He nodded toward Brett. "I know it's a risky strategy,
but I've been watching him. On his last two trips to the
line, between shots, he leans forward, his hands pulling
on the bottom of his shorts. He's dead tired, and his
form is breaking down."

Cody paused and looked to his coach. Coach
Clayton didn't return Cody's look, but he did say,
"You heard your captain."

After Berringer missed a long baseline jumper, Macy snagged the rebound and charged downcourt. Cody scrambled to stay with him, but he fell for a hesitation move and Macy knifed toward the basket from the left wing. "Help!" Cody called.

Goddard left his man and turned his attention to Macy, slapping him across the forearm as he released the ball. Macy left the shot short but smiled as he strutted to the line for two free throws.

He drank in a deep breath and released his first shot. Cody smacked his hands together as Macy short-armed the attempt. He pounded the ball angrily against the hardwood as he prepared for try number two. Over-compensating for the first miss, Macy clanged this one off the back iron. Leaping quickly, Brett snagged the rebound and fired the outlet pass to Gannon.

Gannon took the ball down the middle, where Tucker, Central's hulking power forward—fouled him before he could get off a shot.

Gannon missed the front end of the one-and-one, and Macy walked the ball upcourt after Miller's rebound.

"They're gonna take the air out of the ball," Cody barked to his teammates. "Get up on 'em! Pressure 'em!"

The Eagles' ball-hawking defense forced turnovers on two of the next three Central possessions. However, it also earned Brett Evans his fifth foul and a seat on the bench next to Slaven.

The scoreboard stood frozen at 43–41 as the game entered its final minute. Macy posted up Cody in the low block and fired up one of his patented jump hooks. The ball was halfway through the hoop when it popped back out, as if regurgitated.

Berringer darted back and forth across the baseline on Grant's ensuing possession, finally freeing himself for a jumper from the left side. But his shot rattled out.

Tucker got free on a back pick and could have put the Grizzlies up by four, but he missed a point-blank layup. Hooper screened out Miller, who, in frustration, swatted the ball out of his hands.

Cody studied the game clock. Only eighteen seconds remained, with the Eagles still down by two. *Gotta end this thing now*, he thought. *With Matt and Brett gone—and Hoop carrying four fouls—we'd probably get killed in overtime.*

He stood on the end line waiting to inbound the ball to Gannon. It looked like Central was going to pick up their defense at half-court. "G," he said, "look for me on the left wing. My guy's been giving me some room."

Gannon nodded. Cody could only hope it wasn't an obligatory nod—and that Gannon didn't plan to launch a three-pointer from deep downtown and make himself the hero.

As soon as Gannon got the ball, Macy sprinted across half-court to pressure him. Cody swallowed hard. Gannon wasn't the most careful ball handler, and Macy had been playing like a wildcat the whole game.

"You got help behind ya!" Cody called.

Gannon wheeled and lobbed an underhand pass to Cody. Cody looked ahead and saw nothing but open court in front of him. He pushed the ball up the right side of the court, waiting for a defender to pick him up. But Tucker sagged off of him, daring him to shoot.

Cody stole another look at the clock. Eleven seconds left. *Well*, he told himself, *here goes nothin'. A three-point play would be nice.*

He veered toward the basket at a forty-five-degree angle. Tucker stood planted in front of him like a tree. Cody moved around his defender, disappointed that he couldn't bait him into a foul. Still, if he hit a layup, there would be time to—

Cody was unable to finish his thought, as Miller, rumbling across the lane, slammed into him. Falling backward, Cody tried to compensate for the contact and lofted a looping right-handed scoop shot toward the hoop.

From a seated position on the floor, he watched the ball circle the rim once—then curl out.

"Good hard foul!" Macy said, slapping Miller across the rump. "So much for their three-point play."

Goddard grabbed Cody by the wrist and pulled him to his feet. "Almost, man. *Almost*," he said.

Cody studied the clock. Four seconds remained. "It's not over, G." he said. "Keep your head in the game."

"Two shots, gentlemen," Cody heard the referee say as he positioned himself at the line. "Relax on the first one."

Relax? Cody marveled. *Easy for you to say.*

He planted his feet at shoulder width. He eyed the rim and made sure his right elbow was straight. With a flick of the wrist, the ball left his hand. *Okay, there's one point,* he said to himself as the ball snapped through the net. *Now, do I tie it, or do we go for the win—tell Central it's time to start the bus?*

He stole a quick glance at Coach Clayton, who brought his forefinger up and touched his nose. The signal to leave his second shot short. Cody followed the exact routine of his first shot. However, he stopped his follow-through at its midpoint, rather than letting his hand "follow" the ball toward the basket.

The ball caromed off the front of the rim. Cody saw Macy dart in front of him to block his path to the basket, but Macy was a moment too late. Cody swiveled his hips and curled in front of Macy. He leaped and extended his arms. The ball drifted slightly to the left, so, with his left hand, he nudged it softly back toward the rim.

The follow-up shot dropped through cleanly.

Come on, buzzer! Cody thought.

Instead, he heard a whistle. Macy had turned to the nearest official and signaled a time-out—with two seconds left.

As Cody ran toward Coach Clayton, he felt hands clapping him across the back. "Sweet follow, Code!" he heard someone say. He whipped around and stared down his smiling teammates. "Gotta wipe those grins off, fellas," he scolded. "This isn't over."

"Fall back! Fall back on defense!" Brett Evans exhorted the team as they approached the bench. "Don't foul, whatever you do, and we can finally win one!"

Coach Clayton looked at Cody. "Well, captain, do you agree with Brett?"

Cody thought for a moment. "Nah, Coach. Not this time. We gotta pressure the inbounds pass. Lang, you stick on Macy like gum. Goddard, you lay off Tucker a little bit. I'll get right up in Miller's grill when he tries to inbound. When he sees Macy's locked up, he'll go to Tucker. Then, G, you get to the ball before Tucker does."

Goddard looked like he was trying to swallow a jumbo egg, shell and all. "But I don't know if I'm fast enough," he said.

Cody shook his head violently. "No. You *get* fast enough."

Coach Clayton looked at Cody and smiled. "Well," he said, "you heard your captain."

Cody stood in front of Miller, hopping up and down and extending his arms over his head. However, he shaded just to the big center's right, on the same side of the court where Macy was going through a series of stop-and-go moves trying to shake free of Lang. On the left side of the court, Goddard stood about ten feet from Tucker, looking away from him. Cody saw panic in Miller's eyes as he looked in Macy's direction. Cody scooted even farther to Miller's right. "Five seconds!" he called, reminding Miller that he needed to inbound the ball—immediately.

Desperate, Miller rotated his torso and snapped a hard chest pass to Tucker. Goddard took two bounding steps, then dove.

He snagged the ball with his right hand, bouncing it once on the hardwood, and, somehow, maintained his dribble even as he belly flopped on the floor.

With the buzzer ringing in his ears, Cody sprinted to Goddard.

"Hey, G," he said tugging his teammate to his feet, "nice catch!"

"I still don't know about my speed," Goddard said, struggling to regain his breath.

"Sometimes, want to is better than speed," Cody observed.

Pork Chop was on the court even before Coach Clayton and Cody's teammates jumped up from the bench. "That was good," he said, beaming, "that was stupid-good! Man, I wish we were playing together!"

As soon as those words were out, Cody saw the joy leave his friend's eyes. They stood silent for a moment, and Cody sensed they both knew Pork Chop's wish transcended just the current hoops season.

"Whatever happens," Cody said, his voice ragged, "we'll always be teammates. If not in sports, in life."

Epilogue

Cody finished his Sunday-morning devotions by reading Isaiah 41:10: "Do not fear, for I am with you; do not be dismayed, for I am your God."

He closed his Bible, using Robyn's poem as a bookmark.

He heard his dad and Beth laughing and talking downstairs. Sometimes he would wake to this sound and think his mom was alive. When reality hit, it was bittersweet. The sweet was that his dad was finally happy again. *The bitter—well, I don't even want to think about that*, he reminded himself.

Cody squirmed in the pew as Pastor Taylor began his closing illustration. *Uh-oh,* he thought. *This is gonna be rough.*

He had heard the story before, during Pastor Taylor's Easter service a year or two ago. It had made him cry then—and he hadn't had nearly as much to cry over as he did now. He feared a repeat meltdown, and there was no easy exit to the restroom.

He was trapped. In the middle of a pew. Sandwiched between his dad and Beth on one side and burly Mr. Porter on the other.

"The fire was out of control," Pastor Taylor was saying. "It was too hot for the father to run back into the house. And the sound of the sirens was far away. The fire trucks wouldn't get there in time.

"So the father stood under the second-story window, pleading with his five-year-old son: "Please, Michael, you have to jump. Just jump. I'll catch you."

Cody swallowed hard. He knew what was coming next.

"Michael, framed by the open window, looked down toward his father's voice. But he couldn't see him for all the smoke. 'But, Daddy,' he cried. 'Where are you? I can't see you! I can't see you!'

"Michael's father, battling back tears, looked up at his son. 'I know Michael,' he said, his voice strong and clear. 'But I can see you. And I will catch you. I promise.'"

Cody looked to his left. Beth was sniffling, swirling her hand about inside her purse. Fishing for a tissue, no doubt.

Cody closed his eyes tightly. *As long as my eyes are closed*, he told himself, *no tears can leak out. So keep 'em closed, Martin. Keep 'em closed tight.*

He heard Pastor Taylor clear his throat. His voice took on the trembling, slightly wounded quality it always did at moments like this. "Some of you are just like the little boy Michael," he said. "Life has driven you to the edge. The flames are at your back. Smoke surrounds you. You can barely breathe. You long to jump into the safety of God's loving arms, but you can't see him. You're blinded. By pain. By confusion. By uncertainty. By loss. But God sees you."

The pastor paused for a moment. "He sees you, Blake Randall. He sees you, Councilwoman Reynolds. He sees you, dear Mr. Sanders. He sees you, Cody Martin."

Cody felt tears slipping from his eyes. He felt one arm around his shoulders, then another. He heard the pew in back of him groan slightly as someone leaned forward and patted the back of his head.

The tears were coming faster now, but Cody ceased caring about them—or trying to stop them. Each one that trickled down his face seemed to take some of the pain with it. The pain of Chop moving away. Of his dad remarrying. Of the gash in his heart left by his mom's death.

Cody opened his eyes when he heard the music. Pastor Taylor had relinquished the podium to the small contemporary worship band. Cody felt himself smile slightly as he recognized the song. *This is a good one*, he thought, as he stood. *dc Talk. Old school.*

He felt a small hand light on his left shoulder and give it a soft squeeze. He looked behind him to see Jill Keller smiling at him. He nodded at her and turned his attention to the band again. "I took a dive," they sang. "I took a love plunge into your arms—"

Okay, God, he prayed. *I got the message. All this stuff I'm dealing with, the pressure, the uncertainty, the pain—I'm giving it all to you. I just can't stand up to all of it on my own anymore. You're my only hope.*

Cody felt his body growing weak, as if his leg bones were turning to rubber. He listed to his left, leaning against his dad. His father was lean, probably not weighing more than Cody, but his body felt like a tree, firmly rooted. On his right, he felt Mr. Porter wrap one of his bridge-cable arms around his shoulder. Leah Taylor, the pastor's wife, turned around in the pew ahead and took both of Cody's hands in hers. "We got ya, Cody," she whispered.

Cody, realizing now that he was standing with a strength not his own, thought back to all the times his mom had told him, "My one and only son, we have an awesome privilege: We get to be God's hands and feet. We can do work for those who aren't able to. We can bring the touch of kindness and compassion. And when someone falls, God can use us to catch them."

Cody had understood those words. Now he was *feeling* them. Living them. He looked up to the church rafters. "Hey, God," he whispered. "Nice catch."

Acknowledgments

Big, shiny MVP awards to the following people:

Bruce, Robin, Kristen, and everyone at Zonderkidz for believing in this series.

The Mill Valley High School football and basketball teams for reminding this has-been ex-jock how the games are played in the twenty-first century.

My YMCA League teams—the Super Saiyans, the Legend, the Vikings, and the Dragons—for the privilege of coaching you and for the many lessons you have taught me about sportsmanship and courage.

Barbara Scott for your strong, early support of Cody and his story. There wouldn't be a book, and certainly not a whole series, if not for you.

Toby Mac for penning the foreword to this series. You captured The Spirit of the Game perfectly.

Jami Hafer for the poem, "For a Friend."

Dave Dravecky for the athletic expertise and the spiritual wisdom you have shared with me through conversation and the fine books you have written.

Tim Hanson for being my teammate, and more importantly, my friend through so many seasons of sports and of life. Even though we weren't able to coauthor this series as I had hoped, your mark is on every book. And every life that this series touches, every accomplishment it inspires, I share with you.